UNEXPECTED ASSIGNMENT

GUARDING THE ANTICHRIST

A Novel By:

MICHAEL VILARDI

ISBN: 979-8-9998482-4-6
ISBN: 979-8-9998482-5-3

For more information and to view other books by this author, please visit
www.MikeVilardi.com

A book written to help the readers understand the second coming of Christ and the events leading up to it.

DEDICATION

This book is dedicated to the memory of my Junior High School Wrestling and Cross-Country Coach, Robert Klement. Bob was a true winner. During my years in junior high, from 1972 to 1974, Bob's cross-country team won every race they ran over those three years. In wrestling, they won every match but one, and that single loss was only because our best wrestlers, including myself, were out sick and could not compete.

I give Coach Klement all the credit for instilling in me a winning attitude that has brought me much success in all that I have done.

I remember the day it happened like it was yesterday. We had a wrestling match against Selden, and I was supposed to wrestle at 88 pounds, but I had a chocolate milk at lunch. At the weigh-in, I was a quarter pound overweight. Coach was upset; he had to put in the second-string kid at 88 pounds and moved me up to 94 pounds to wrestle. Coach was not happy, he was really upset, so I promised him that I would win, no matter what. That day, my attitude changed. It was no longer about there being two of us on the mat with a 50-50 chance; it was about me winning, no matter what. That was the day that changed my life.

I stepped onto the mat against an opponent who was six pounds heavier and three inches taller. It did not matter. I won 13–6, and from that day forward, I wrestled to win. My wrestling ability got me to college and gave me a winning attitude for life.

Years later, I had a television show on cable TV, and I interviewed my friend and co-captain of the high school wrestling team, Chester Gayles. Chester won his first 100 wrestling matches and was a prime example of Coach Klement's coaching ability. Chester had been shot nine times and lived, a true testament to God's grace and mercy. So, we did a TV show about it. We then found Coach and shared the show with him. Subsequently, I did a TV show with Coach and Chester. Coach and I kept in touch until his death.

I remember when I ran for Congress, how he would call me to encourage me. Coach and his wife, Diane, not only supported me with words but with financial contributions to fund my campaign. I will always be grateful for having known Bob and Diane, and their son Jamie.

Robert Klement was truly a winner in life and all that he did.

Special thanks to Tom Holohan, a great friend and pastor, for his time and effort in editing this book. Tom spent weeks coming to my house to edit this book. He was the driving force behind me writing this novel. I will always remember his time and effort spent helping me with this endeavor. Additional special thanks to Nick Nicols, Tindra Lanfrank, Rita Shafeek, and Ivette Brown, who assisted me in the final edit.

Special thanks to Rev. Tim for writing the foreword and for being a friend. For more information, please visit www.DamonLegna.com. His nonprofit organization is changing the world. Please visit the website and see for yourself.

Additional love to Angeline Vilardi, Jeremy and Bernadette Pahl, and their wonderful daughter, Marie. I also want to thank my son, Jeffrey, for being a great son and someone I can always count on. There is nothing better than having a great relationship with your son. It makes a father proud.

To my cousins, whom I love with all my heart: Linda Fazio, Tindra Lanfrank, Joey Fazio, Michele Lanfrank, Linda Jo Benedetto, Camielle Johnston,

Patti Tierno, Tindra Redmond, Joseph Castagna, Billy Paparelli, Cecilia and John Anthony, Nicholas Benedetto, and, of course, my cousin Vinny Venditto. To my Uncle Al and Aunt Marie, I could not have chosen a better uncle.

I pray that if you haven't done so already, you make Jesus Lord of your life.

To my favorite college friends: Ned Futterman, Greg Goldstein, Joe Tringali, and Paul Friedman (rest in peace, my friend).

To all the children at GRC Orphanage in Pakistan. Pastor Imran Razzaq, I thank you for the opportunity to preach in Pakistan and for all the beautiful children you take care of there. The kids are truly precious. Gennaro DiNapoli, thank you for your friendship and support for the orphans.

To two of my favorite supervisors at the IRS, Jay Grossett and Tom DiStefano, thank you for your leadership and inspiration.

I can't forget my other closest friends: Rita Shafeek, Tommy and Bella Holohan, Costos Mandylor, Pat Farrell, Ralph D'Arcy, Renee Wiggins, Bill Brent, Alan and Ivette Brown, Brendan and Sandi Kelly, Rev. Tim, Kelly Lefaivre, Mark Restivo, Elsa Figueras, Joseph Gourlay, Ian Gardner, John Faro, Terry Wise, Annie Delgado, Rosemarie Frigerio, Bob Wallace and his wife Genie, Neil Cohen, Scott Cayouette, Mary Piersall, William McNamara, Liz Felton, Gene Giuliano, Joe Crocetti, Ed Lynch, and Craig Webkie. There are many more for whom I am truly thankful.

❖

Michael Vilardi

FOREWORD

When I first met Mike Vilardi in 2012, his personality was infectious. People just seemed to love being around him. He has unique characteristics of Honesty, Integrity, and Trust which are rare today. As a retired Federal Agent, Mike faced many dangers, and gives glory to God for keeping him safe throughout his illustrious career. You see, Mike stands on the Living Word of God, because he studies it with a fervent hunger like no other.

Mike has a Spiritual Gift of understanding. He's able to digest the Word of God, then deliver it to others in an easy-to-understand charismatic way. Throughout this book, you will be given insight to what some view as the complex Biblical topic of Salvation. God's Words says the day and hour of the Lord's return is unknown (Matthew 24:36), but Mike outlines the many clues and parables which were left for us to discern. It's truly a Blessing to know God is still seeking his lost sheep.

Reverend Tim

CONTENTS

INTRODUCTION

I entitled this book "Unexpected Assignment: Guarding the Anti-Christ" because I want people to understand that God has a plan for coming back to planet earth to redeem and restore it. The Bible tells us that Jesus will reign on the earth for 1000 years, then God will create a new heaven and a new earth for eternity.

Most people do not understand God's plan for redeeming the earth. I hope to answer the question of when Jesus is coming back and why it is soon! All of my answers come from the Bible with my commentary and understanding.

Simply stated, Jesus is coming back to restore and redeem the earth to the state it was before the fall of man. The book of Revelation details the events that lead up to his return.

The event that starts the clock ticking is the event known as the catching up of the saints. Where Paul the apostle wrote that the dead in Christ shall rise first and those that are alive will be caught up to be with him.

1 Thessalonians 4:14-18

14 For since we believe that Jesus died and was raised to life again, we also believe that when Jesus returns, God will bring back with him the believers who have died.

15 We tell you this directly from the Lord: We who are still living when the Lord returns will not meet him ahead of those who have died.

16 For the Lord himself will come down from heaven with a commanding shout, with the voice of the archangel, and with the trumpet call of God. First, the believers who have died will rise from their graves.

17 Then, together with them, we who are still alive and remain on the earth will be caught up in the clouds to meet the Lord in the air. Then we will be with the Lord forever.

18 So encourage each other with these words.

This event begins the clock ticking. From the time God takes half his saints to heaven, "one will be taken, one will be left" as Jesus said in:

Matthew 24:40-43 NKJV
Then two men will be in the field: one will be taken and the other left. 41 Two women will be grinding at the mill: one will be taken and the other left. 42 Watch therefore, for you do not know what hour your Lord is coming.

From the time of this event, there will be ten and a half years before the return of Christ to rule on earth.

This book will be a short exposé on the first three and a half years following the Rapture, which is the tribulation time for the saints, then comes Daniel's 70th week, which is the last 7 years before his return. However, it is being written from the perspective of one living through it. That is why I use a diary format. I hope this makes it readable and enjoyable for you, the reader.

For a more thorough analysis, I recommend my book – "The Time of His Coming 2" – The Final Chapter" and "The Key to Understanding Revelation" by Arthur E. Bloomfield.

I hope you enjoy the book and gain a better understanding of what the Bible predicts for the future.

CHAPTER 1
BOB DREAMS OF HEAVEN

Before we begin to tell the story of Bob's diary we need to begin with the characters in the book.

Before I will introduce our characters, who will help us live through the period of time the bible calls the great tribulation period, which lasts 1260 days and begins immediately after the faithful Christians are caught up to heaven and ends 1260 days later in Revelation 7:9 when they are all seen in heaven. I want to explain the 3 distinct periods of tribulation that occur after the overcoming Christians are caught up to heaven, an event also known as the rapture.

First, we have a 1260 period of time that occurs immediately after the rapture of the Christians. During this time 4 things happen. First a war in heaven, where Satan and all his demons are cast down to earth. At this point Satan takes over the body of the Anti-Christ and seems to rise from the dead. The false prophet will tell the world he is the messiah and the turmoil begins.

Then we see the 4 seal judgments being released: war, inflation, famine and death. The Anti-Christ will take over the European common market nations and wax great. He will demand that no one can buy or sell anything without the mark of the beast, which means that you worship him alone as your god.

The 3rd thing that will happen during this period of time is that the gospel (Revelation 14:6) will be preached to every human being by the saints that were transformed at the rapture. God will pour out his spirit on all flesh, so no one can say that they didn't hear it or feel it. The 4th thing is found in Ezekiel 38 and 39. A war in Israel, where at least 6 nations invade, including Russia, Iran and Turkey. These nations thinking they will destroy Israel are suddenly destroyed by the greatest earthquake in recorded history. As this happens God seals 144,000 Jews from his judgments to come. Everyone who accepted the gospel of Jesus Christ is caught up to heaven; we see them there in Revelation 7:9. Finally the government of Israel moves in fear and agrees to a peace treaty with the Anti-Christ to begin Daniel's 70th week but as he puts his pen to the paper God fulfills Ezekiel 39:9 where the people of Israel use the left-over weapons for fuel for 7 years. This is done as a constant reminder of what God did for Israel.

This period of time is followed by a period of time known as Daniel's 70th week, which is the final seven years before the return of Christ. The first half of this period of time is marked by the Trumpet judgments of God that destroy 1/3 of the world's land mass with fire, 1/3 of the oceans and the rivers as God judges a world that refused his grace and mercy and persecuted and killed his saints. Israel builds the temple during this period too. The 2nd half of Daniel's 70th week begins when the Anti-Christ goes into the temple and declares himself as God, then God reacts by sending his 2 witnesses to earth, Enoch and Isaiah, the only 2 people that did not die. The Anti-Christ then invades Israel and kills the 2 witnesses and conquers half of Jerusalem. It is at that point that Christ comes with his army and takes back the earth.

The false prophet and the Anti-Christ are thrown into the Lake of Fire and Satan is bound 1000 years. Now the Kingdom of God begins. This is a simple summary of the major events that occur.

Let's learn a bit about our characters. First, Bob Klement. He is a 25-year-old graduate student, studying business marketing at a college on Long Island. He is a good Catholic; he was an altar boy from the time he was 10 till he was 13. He faithfully goes to church and confession. He is a good guy and well-liked by all who know him.

Diana is Bob's study partner. She is 23 years old and also a graduate student. Diana is a born again Christian and is engaged to be married. Diana got engaged 6 months ago and moved in with her boyfriend Larry after they announced their engagement. They plan to marry in May 2029. Larry manages a car dealership, makes good money and is very likable though Diana thought he was a good catch and didn't want him to get away. Larry insisted that they live together before they get married so that they could work out any differences before the wedding. Larry doesn't believe in God and saw no problem with it though Diana thought it would be ok since they were already acting as man and wife and they planned to get married anyway.

Brace yourself; you are about to experience the Tribulation period from the pages of Bob's diary.

Let us begin the journey with Bob's dream on the night of September 3rd 2028.

It was a Tuesday night at 2 am; I was lying in bed asking God to show me the things that would happen in the future. I asked him to show me the events in the book of revelation. As I prayed, I dozed off to sleep, but was awaked when I heard a voice say,

"Come up here and I will show you things that must take place."

Before I knew it, I was in heaven standing on streets of Gold. I looked up, a female angel in a gloried body that glowed, welcomed me to heaven. Her name was Angeline; she was beautiful in form and features. I knew her name just by looking at her. In heaven you don't have to talk, but it is nice when you do. Angeline told me that she was my guide that she would show me the things that the Lord wanted me to know. Her beauty amazed me and she read my thoughts. She said,

"Everyone was beautiful there, you are in heaven."

I asked why I was there. But before she could answer, Michael the Arc Angel entered the street and approached us. Michael was on his way to meet the Lord at the throne room, which I could see in the distance. Michael said,

"The time was short and all the preparations were being made for the saints of God to be transformed into their glorified bodies."

With that he left us. Angeline said,

"First I must take you to meet Paul."

I said,

"The Paul from the bible?"

Angeline said,

"Yes that Paul."

She took my hand and we were transported to this beautiful Mansion on a hill. We entered the home to see a young man in his glorified body; all people look young in heaven. The apostle Paul introduced himself. I humbled myself before him. He said,

"When I was among men, the Lord brought me here and showed me the things that are about to take place. I was humbled with a thorn in my side so that my pride would not destroy me. When you leave here remember to humble yourself."

I agreed that I would. Paul explained that three things must occur before the rapture (the event that transforms Christians into their glorified bodies) can take place. Reminding me that immediately after the rapture Satan will be cast to the earth; when that happens, he will lose his ability to access the heavens. Paul then continued,

"First, the European market nations will consolidate its leadership. This will set the stage for his coming. Secondly, a unity religion between Islam, Buddha, Hindu and Catholics will begin to evolve. This will eventually create the largest religion known to man. The leader of this religion will proclaim the Anti-Christ the caliphate (the leader the Muslim's have been waiting for) so this must be done before his coming."

Paul then looked at me and said,

"Religion is the biggest obstacle keeping people from salvation. That is why thou shall have no gods before me is the first and most important commandment."

Because of this religious unity a false peace will come upon the earth that will be destroyed when the Devil and his demons are cast down from the heavens to the earth.

"Thirdly," Paul continued, "people will be talking of peace and safety, so it will be a time of relative peace. When I was on the earth, I wrote to the Thessalonians explaining to them that the brethren would not be in darkness like the rest of the world. The reason I wrote this is because the three things I am telling you now must take place before the rapture and before Satan can be cast to the earth. The devil will have a body that is ready to be possessed by him. Remember Satan rebelled against God because he wanted to be worshiped like him. So, he tries to imitate God, since Jesus overcame death, the devil will try to do the same thing. However, the person Satan will possess will not have died. He will be brain dead but not dead until Satan possesses his body and brings him back to life. Finally, the most important sign is that the person who becomes the Anti-Christ must get a deadly head wound. When you see that happen you are at the door, even though no one will know the day or hour, you will know within a short time of this event occurring."

Paul continued,

"We are preparing for this event now in heaven, it will soon be happening on earth. Now go back and tell the brothers to watch and pray!"

With that Angeline took me by the hand and we left. Angeline said,

"I want you to meet Peter before you go back to earth."

So, we were transported to a field where Peter was standing. Peter saw us and said,

"Welcome to heaven."

Then he said,

"My time with you will be short. Remember that a day is to the Lord as a thousand years, and since the creation of Adam six thousand years has passed. We here in heaven are preparing for the soon return of the Lord. Go now and tell the world that the time of his coming is at the door."

With that I found myself back in my bed. I looked at the clock and it was 4am. I couldn't sleep so I got a piece of paper and wrote it all down. I will have to speak to Diana about this because she is more spiritual than I am.

CHAPTER 2
THE RAPTURE

CHRISTIANS GET CAUGHT UP TO HEAVEN

Monday September 4th, 2028

I walked into the campus center to meet Diana to study. When I saw her, I noticed that she was arguing with another woman. As I approached the table, the woman walked away, right past me. She was attractive but had a very aggravated look on her face as she passed by. She said nothing to me as she passed me. When I sat down next to Diana, I asked her who the woman was. She said,

"It was my friend Denise."

I asked what the argument was about. Diana said,

"Denise was upset with me because I moved in with Larry."

Diana explained that she was telling Denise how Larry expects her to clean the house, make dinner, do his laundry and just takes her for granted. Denise told her it would be a mistake to move in with Larry and now, Diana regrets it. The two of us finally sat down to study graduate financial reporting, an advanced accounting course. I want a law enforcement job when I graduate and I remember my father telling me that most crimes are financial so you better understand accounting and finances. I took my father's advice and studied accounting. As Diana and I studied I told her that I was thinking of going to work with the Secret Service or FBI when I graduate. She seemed a bit distant while I was talking to her, I think she was preoccupied with the way Larry has been treating her. We studied hard and felt confident that we would do well in the course. Since I noticed she was preoccupied I decided to hold off talking about last night's dream.

Bob's diary

Monday September 11, 2028

Today was the strangest day of my life. I was in New York to mark the anniversary of 9/11; my friend Diana asked me to go with her because her father died in tower one that day. I went with her. On the way there I told her about the dream I had, how I was taken to heaven to meet Paul and Peter. She said,

"I thought it was odd that Assad of Syria was attacked last week when he tried to get back into power in Syria. He has been on life support for a week already."

Diana didn't believe he could be the Anti-Christ and said,

"People have been talking about this for thousands of years and nothing ever happened. It was only a dream and not to worry about it."

After the ceremonies Larry came to meet us for dinner and take Diana home. It was 6pm when we left the restaurant and I began the drive back to Long Island alone. I was on the BQE (Brooklyn, Queens Expressway) when I noticed an attractive woman driving next to me. She looked sophisticated, beautiful dark hair, big brown eyes and a nice smile. I kept looking over at her. She had what looked like her Italian grandmother in the front seat next to her. Her grandmother was yelling at her for something, but I couldn't tell what it was.

Then it happened, out of nowhere; an ear-piercing trumpet blast, it was so loud I thought I was hearing a concert from heaven. As the trumpets sounded, I looked up and I could see these gold portals in the sky. Before I knew it, I could see people ascending into the sky and going through those gold portals. It amazed me, in total disbelief. Then I looked over to see that beautiful woman that was driving next to me, and she was gone! Her grandmother grabbed the wheel and her car was coming into my lane. I sped up to avoid being hit by her, as I did, a blue Cadillac with no driver cut me off and I rear-ended the car. The car lost control and plunged over the guard rail and I could hear it crash to the ground below. I didn't know what was happening so I got off the highway and took local streets back to Long Island, it took hours. Those trumpets kept blasting for about 20 minutes, people kept going into those portals and then I heard them stop. As soon as they stopped the portals disappeared.

But as I drove, I went past a cemetery and I could see that dirt had exploded out of the ground and I saw a man dressed in white, a young-looking man with a glow about him that suddenly came out of one of the graves.

All I kept thinking was this must be a terrorist attack, it is 9/11 what else could it be? (I totally forgot about the dream from the other night).

I saw a car hit a hydrant at 30 miles an hour and the driver was gone. I was seeing people's clothes all over the streets. Underwear, sneakers, jeans, shirts scattered all over the road. Did the terrorists develop a new weapon that can zap people and make them disappear? I did not know. All I knew was that there was chaos everywhere. No one seemed to know what had just happened. After, I got home (3 hours later) I immediately called my friend Diana, my cell phone didn't work, all circuits were busy. So, I decided to run over to her house, she only lives a mile away. So, I grabbed a flashlight and began the trek. Twenty minutes later I was knocking on her door.

Chaos ruled the day. On the way over, I saw looting, people outside screaming. One teenage girl was crying,

"My Mom is gone, my mom is gone, help me, and help me!"

The panic was unlike anything I have ever seen. Larry opened the door and said,

"I am glad you are all right, come on in."

I entered the house and asked where Diana was. Larry said,

"She was upstairs crying uncontrollably, but I will tell her you are there."

While I was waiting, I heard this big explosion. I ran outside frantically and what do I see: a small plane hit a home that was 4 houses away, and fire is burning everywhere. What else could happen? This has to be a terrorist attack or was this what my dream was all about. I ran back into the house and there Diana was with a tissue in her hand drying her eyes. I told her,

"This has to be the greatest terror attack in the world's history."

She stopped crying looked me straight in the eye and said,

"No Bob, this is no terror attack."

I said,

"Then what is it?"

She said,

"Bob, this is the greatest miracle that the Bible records. This is the event that Jesus spoke about when he said two men will be in a bed, one will be taken and one will be left, two women would be in the field one will be taken and one will be left. Watch and pray that you are accounted worthy. That is what this event is."

Diana explained that this is the event depicted in Revelation 12:5, where the child is caught up to God. Diana further explained that my dream was happening! I know nothing about the Bible so I asked Diana,

"If you know all this why didn't you go?"

Then Diana cried again, and explained that she wanted to be with Larry so badly that she compromised her morals and moved in with him. Diana said,

"This was for the overcomers and explained a parable found in Matthew 25 about the ten virgins. Five had oil in their lamps and five did not. The ones without the oil stayed behind, and I was one of those."

Then she started crying uncontrollably again. I could not stand it; I had to leave. I got home and passed out.

CHAPTER 3
THE AFTERMATH

Tuesday September 12, 2028

I woke up today to the news that the President declared a state of emergency. He called a news conference and said that there are 24 million people worldwide have been reported missing since yesterday. The president called for calm and said that Pope Peter will be speaking at the Vatican tomorrow to explain what happened yesterday. I was so depressed I spent the day in bed watching TV. I put on the news and watched the newscaster interview different people that saw people who were taken to heaven. The first interview was of a 16-year-old boy. The boy said that he shared a room with his 14-year-old brother and they were both in the room playing video games, when they heard an ear-piercing trumpet blast. Then suddenly his brother Mark was gone. All that was left was his clothes. The next lady was a nurse; she was taking care of a patient in the hospital when the Dr. walked in to check the man's chart. She heard an ear-piercing trumpet blast and then the Dr. was gone. Only his clothes were left behind. The third guy they spoke to was a construction worker. He was on a construction site finishing up for the day when they heard the trumpet blast then the bulldozer operator was gone and the bulldozer kept moving. They couldn't believe it; all that was left was the man's clothes inside the bulldozer.

After 2 hours of hearing the similar stories over and over I had to go to bed. Maybe someone will have a better explanation tomorrow.

Wednesday September 13, 2028

I finally got out of bed. I decided to go for a run. I got out there to run at about noon and I immediately noticed it was freezing. It was weird but I started my run. I did not get too far...then I heard the loudest thunder EVER. Sounded like Zeus and the Greek gods were fighting in heaven, but I doubt that was it. Then a darkness that was oppressive and hard to explain seemed to blanket the earth. I could feel an evil that I cannot even describe. As I was contemplating what was happening, I saw a being, a huge spirit being hit the earth. It was like a missing link, huge but you could see through it. I got scared and ran home. I called Diana in a panic. I got through. I pleaded with her to explain to me what was happening. Diana noticed the evil presence as well, she then said,

"This is the event found in Revelation 12:7-9, that the Devil and his demons have been cast down to the earth. From this point on things will be very different on planet Earth."

Diana said that the Pope would be speaking soon. I got off the phone with Diana and turned on the Television.

Pope Peter was just coming to the podium. He began to speak saying,

"Citizens of the World, I am here today to bring calm to all of you. Two days ago, millions of people disappeared. I know everyone is wondering why. So today, I am here to explain to the world what happened. For the last several years I and my predecessor have been trying to bring the world together by creating a unity religion. On March 15th of this year, as you know, we agreed. The Catholics, Muslims, Hindus, Buddhists and almost every other major religion except the Jews and those people that consider themselves born again Christians all agreed. Under that agreement that we signed in March, I, Pope Peter will lead the Unity church from Rome but Sharia law shall govern the religion. It also included other provisions for the other religions that joined so that we could bring peace to a world divided by religious conflict. Since that time a lot has happened, we changed the churches and Mosques throughout the world to reflect our unity. Religious conflicts throughout the world decreased by 90% because of this. Now, I will explain what happened 2 days ago. The god of this world, Allah the wonderful, took from the earth all those who refused to be part of the Unity Religion. Let me clarify, he only took the most zealous ones, giving the others a second chance to come home to our unified faith. The haters are gone, so we can enjoy a peace on earth that has never been seen before. Allah, the wonderful, has reincarnated himself in the form of the president of Assyria. If you remember two weeks ago today, a rebel with a hunting knife brutally attacked the president of Assyria. The rebel stabbed him in the head and for the last 2 weeks he was brain dead on life support. Just 6 hours ago, he came back from the dead. He is more vibrant now, than ever before, ready to rule this world. On Saturday, he will address all the people of the world at 2pm. I have declared him the caliphate (the leader that Islam has been waiting for) and ask all members of the Unity church to worship and honor him alone. To prove that what I am saying is true, I have planned a special event at the Vatican that will take place at 6pm on Saturday after the president speaks. For now, I say do not worry, the haters are gone and Allah has come to the earth in the form of the Assyrian president. Miracles will follow to show you this is true. Good night."

When Pope Peter concluded speaking, I was more confused than ever. Could it be true that all those people were taken because of their refusal to join the Unity church? I am too tired to ponder the thought. I am off to bed.

Friday September 15th, 2028

The Assyrian President addressed the World today and everyone watched. You could see there was something different about him. His eyes looked fierce, the way he carried himself and the way he spoke. This was not the same man that allowed rebels to divide his country. He began,

"Citizens of the world, you know that 2 weeks ago I was attacked by a Syrian rebel that stabbed me in the head and left me for dead. But the brave men that surround me took me to a hospital and saved my life. For 2 weeks I lay brain dead in the hospital, then something happened. I was given a vision that seemed like I was there. I saw all the kingdoms of the world, the first great kingdom of Assyria, The pomp of Egypt, The greatness of Babylon and Greece. Then I saw Rome in all her Glory. A man that looked like a god said to me, 'Would you like all the glory of these kingdoms and more.' I said, 'Who are you sir.' He said, 'I am Allah the wonderful, the god of this world.' I asked why he would offer all this to me. He said, 'I am coming to create a kingdom greater than any before it but I need to inhabit the body of a man. You are that man. You are brain dead with no hope of recovery and you are the president of a country. If you give me your body, I will raise you from the dead and the world will see the greatest miracle ever. Then I will do exploits the world has never seen. The kingdom that you will control will be the greatest kingdom man has ever seen. Will you submit to me?' I humbled myself before Allah and said, 'Yes, use me I am yours.' Then I came back to life and I was smarter and stronger than any time before in my life. Now I know that I am to rule the world. Several days ago, the unbelievers were taken out of the way so that I could come and create the greatest kingdom the world has ever seen. My followers are spread throughout the world; I am the caliphate you have been awaiting. I ask the entire world to unite behind me to bring forth a one world government and religion. Then we can have peace on earth. Tonight at 6pm Pope Peter will speak from the Vatican. He will perform miracles that only God can do and instruct you in what needs to be done."

Could this be true? I didn't know. It sounded good but something didn't seem right. I took a nap and set my alarm for 6 pm; I got up and turned on the TV to see Pope Peter speak.

The Vatican overflowed with people. When Pope Peter came out the crowd went wild. I never heard such applause. Pope Peter began,

"For the last 6 months we agreed to unite all religions under one banner, the banner of Unity. So, we formed the Unity religion. The other day I pronounced that the president of Assyria is a man embodied by Allah himself. Tonight, to prove that this is true I offer you a miracle not seen for thousands of years. I ask that all cell phone cameras and recording devices turn to the East and watch and see."

Then the cameras turned away from the pope to point east and we could hear the Pope declare,

"Fire, come out of the heavens and onto the earth."

Then we heard a loud thunder and Fire came down like lightning and all who saw it were amazed. The Pope did it a second time and then a third and the people were mesmerized.

"Now that you have seen the power of our god, I tell all nations and people of the world to unite with us in bringing peace on earth by joining our Unity religion. For the haters who refuse, you have until January 2, 2029 then our supreme leader will call on beloved followers to rise up and kill all the infidels. For too many years religion caused death and division, all that stops on January 2nd, 2029."

The people applauded and the Pope left to a standing ovation. Now I was more confused than ever and even scared. So, I called Diana. She calmed me down and said,

"Pick me up for church at 10am and we will talk then."

I hung up the phone and went to bed.

Sunday September 17th, 2028

I picked up Diana and we headed to church. She belongs to a big church, about 2000 members. We got there 15 mins before the service started but the place was packed. People were parking in the streets to get in. Everyone was there to find out what happened on Tuesday night. When we entered the building, loud music was playing, worship music. The music brought a sense of calm to the church. We found a seat and Pastor Tom came to the podium and announced that he will play worship music for the next 30 mins. As the music played people started to jump and shout, then some people cried and openly confess their sin. Some confessed to sexual immorality, some to drugs and alcohol and others unbelief.

Then Pastor Tom came to the podium and began his sermon.

"For those of you that don't know, the greatest miracle ever recorded happened on Tuesday. The Lord Jesus Christ came for his overcoming saints (those found in Revelation 3:10). Time and time again Jesus taught that 50% would be taken and 50% would be left. He said two will be in the bed one will be taken and one would be left. Two women would be in the field one will be taken and one would be left. That's exactly what happened, look around and you will see that half the church is gone. The question you may ask is why am I here, the answer is simple I did not believe in the rapture and I thought if it did happen all Christians would go. Instead of teaching my church to be overcomers, I excused sin and spoke about God's mercy and grace. Which is why a lot of you are still here? After Tuesday night I spent 3 days in prayer and asked God to show me what to do. Here is what the holy spirit of God showed me: 1) We have exactly 1260 days from September 11th, 2028. Then we will be all be taken up to heaven. You can read about in Revelation 7:9-17. 2) From this time on we will be persecuted by the false prophet, Pope Peter and the Anti-Christ, The president of Assyria. Last night they both gave speeches calling for Unity and they said that they will kill all those that don't comply. The Bible describes the exploits of both these men. Calling fire down from heaven that was told to us in the book of Revelation chapter 13. People that don't know God will believe it. 3) The Anti-Christ will cause wars that lead to starvation and disease that will claim the lives of 25% of the earth's population before we get to the end of the 1260 days, which ends the dispensation of grace. 4) God will pour his spirit out on us so that we can endure the horrors to come. Remember, his kingdom is everlasting. We will rule with him for 1000 years then inhabit a new heaven and earth that is eternal. Let us not lose faith."

Before Pastor Tom could utter another word, we heard a voice from above us say,

"Repent and give God Glory."

The entire church looked up to see a glorified being entering the church from the ceiling and hovering ten feet above us. She looked like a beautiful woman with a heavenly glow about her. Diana turned to me and said,

"Oh my gosh, that is my friend Denise."

Denise was a young 25-year-old virgin that gave Diana a hard time for moving in with Larry and was very critical of their relationship. Diana always gave Denise a hard time for being such a prude and never having any fun. Diana could recognize Denise even with the surrounding glow. Denise told the church,

"The raptured saints will preach the gospel to every human being on the planet. Now that they have their glorified bodies Satan can't stop them."

She explained that they can ascend to heaven and descend to earth. As a result, hundreds of millions of people will accept Christ throughout the world.

"It is the job of the church that was left behind to instruct the new believers in the way of the Lord," she said.

Then she told the church,

"Do not fear."

And left through the ceiling of the church. Pastor Tom then asked anyone that wanted to accept Jesus as their savior to come forward. I went forward and so did half the people that were there, the other half were already Christians that were left behind on Tuesday. What a crazy day.

Monday October 2, 2028

I can't believe how much has changed in such a short time. Demonstrators took to the streets and protested for free healthcare for all, a minimum wage of $35 an hour and government-funded vacations for everyone. Watching these people carry on on television was disturbing. There was a

March by 25,000 people in Washington, demanding free food for all. It got out of hand as they tried to burn the city down to have their demands met! It seems that all the conservatives are gone.

I noticed that evil has increased since last Tuesday and the world has been changed forever!

CHAPTER 4
ELECTION DAY IN THE USA

Tuesday November 7th, 2028

Today was Election Day in the USA and what a day it was. With the Christians gone the democrats did take back the Senate with a 75-seat majority and the House of Representatives with an 83% majority or 361 out of 435 congressmen. The Republicans also lost the presidency as Hillary Harris the female Senator from California, and former VP became the first female President of the USA. In her victory speech she promised Medicare for all, and a ban on the bible. She decried that the bible is too sexist and racist to be legal. Hillary promised to repeal all the executive orders that were put in place by Donald Trump the previous and current President. She promises a socialist utopia! As a result, the stock market sold off very strongly. I got depressed and went to bed.

Thursday November 23, 2028

It is now Thanksgiving. I have not written in a while; it has just been too crazy.

Since September, the world has been absurd. The Christians that were taken in the Rapture had their houses and property looted. The crime in the streets has gotten out of control. The Unity religion is growing and those who refused to join are being ostracized. The economy has suffered because they suddenly took many skilled workers. The good news is that means a lot of jobs are available. The real changes are happening overseas. The president of Assyria has mobilized an invading force into Germany. Last week his army stormed the border under cover of darkness and surprised the German forces. He declared himself the head of the EU

(European Union). On Tuesday the heads of the EU met for an emergency meeting. Seven of the ten decided to yield their power to him. The other three opposed the invasion and vowed to fight. The Prime ministers of Germany and Italy, and the King of Spain tried to convince the others to stand strong and fight. The president of Assyria had asked all his followers to rise up in the name of Allah and fight the oppressors. As a result, the crime in the streets of the EU is out of control; Looting, rape, murder, and demonstrations in every EU nation. The police were helpless to control the situation so the military was called in. Meanwhile, the leaders of the EU convened their Tuesday meeting at 2 am and decided to come back Wednesday at noon to try and hammer out an agreement. But that night something strange happened. All three opposition leaders died mysteriously. The king of Spain died of a heart attack in his sleep. The Prime Minister of Italy died in an elevator when the cable snapped causing the elevator to plunge 23 floors. Then the Prime minister of Germany was shot entering her hotel by a man shouting Allah Akbar. As a result, the president of Assyria announced to the world that he is now the head of the EU, with the other seven leaders agreeing to yield their power to him. He immediately gave a press conference calling for a one world government and one Unity religion. As I watched this on Television you can see the shambles those countries are in and the chaos seems unending.

After watching all this, I had a quiet Thanksgiving at home with Diana. I almost forgot to mention, Larry kicked her out of the house on Halloween. They got into a big fight because she didn't want to be his live-in maid anymore unless they were married. Larry said,

"Screw that."

And packed her bags and put her on the curb. Two weeks later, Larry took in a stripper and she has since moved in with him. Meanwhile, I have allowed Diana to stay in my spare bedroom. I told her we can stay friends but the truth is I am very attracted to her. She is really a looker. The prettiest face I have seen on a woman. I think I am going to bed.

CHAPTER 5
CHRISTMAS EVE

Sunday December 24th 2028 – Christmas Eve

Today was another strange day; Pope Peter announced that instead of celebrating the birth of Christ we should celebrate the resurrection of the Assyrian president. The caliphate is the one that should receive our honor and glory and not Jesus, that's what the Pope said! Then he gave a command and 12 statues that were in St. Peters square came to life at his command. All of them saying,

"Worship him who conquers and does not lose."

Since September he has conquered Europe and many say Africa is next. On a lighter note, Diana and I exchanged gifts. She got me a beautiful Stauer watch and I bought her perfume and clothes. Including a very nice nightgown.

Diana said,

"We need to talk."

So, she explained to me the pain she experienced by being thrown out of the house by Larry, she never wanted to feel like that again. She asked me what my intentions were with her. I told her,

"I think you are the most beautiful woman I know. When I am in your presence, I am happy and content. You have become my best friend and I am in love with you."

She said,

"I love you too but don't want to fall into the same trap I did with Larry. I want to do everything correctly this time, and not go against the word of God."

Diana suggested counseling with Pastor Tom, and I agreed.

Monday December 25th, 2028 Christmas morning

Diana woke me up at 8am to get ready for church. We put on our Christmas best and headed out the door. When we got there the church was packed. While we were in the parking lot getting out of our parked car a group of 3 men drove into the parking lot in a pickup truck. They were carrying rifles and yelling Allah Akbar (which means god is great in Arabic). They approached us with menacing looks in their eyes. The guy in the back of the pickup said,

"Next week at this time, this church will be a Unity church or we will destroy it. You heard the Pope say January 2, 2029 you join us or we kill all you haters!"

Then for good measure he shot out the upstairs windows at the church. As they drove off, they yelled,

"Allah Akbar."

And warned us that they would be back! I stood there in stunned unbelief. Diana was paralyzed with fear. We ran into church once they left to see if they hurt anyone. Thank God, no one was, but the glass was all over the upper floor where we have fellowship after service.

Pastor Tom said,

"Take out your bibles and turn to Luke, Chapter 22:36."

Pastor Tom read it:

"But now, he who has a money bag, let him take it, and likewise a sack; and he who has no sword, let him sell his garment and buy one."

"Now is the time Jesus spoke about when you need to arm yourself. After this morning, I feel we need to protect our families and our property."

Pastor Tom asked the ushers to lock the doors in case those men with guns came back. Then once the doors were locked, we heard a voice in the lobby, yelling,

"Give glory to God, maker of heaven and earth."

Then into the sanctuary walked Ben a raptured saint in his glorified body. He said,

"Stay strong in the Lord and the power of his might."

As he walked through the church and out through the rear wall of the church. I was amazed and mystified at his appearance. After that I could no longer focus on Pastor Tom and before I knew it the church was over. After fellowship upstairs; Diana and I met with pastor Tom for counseling. Diana explained to pastor Tom that we have a strong attraction to each other wanted his relationship advice.

Pastor Tom began by recapping what happened at service. How a raptured saint in his glorified body appeared to us. He said,

"Ben, the saint that appeared to us today came to me 5 years ago to ask advice about whether he should move in with his girlfriend or wait."

Pastor Tom said he would tell us what he told Ben then.

"There are primarily two things that keep people out of the kingdom of God. First and foremost is Religion. If you are religious, you will never have a need for a personal relationship with Christ. You will live your life thinking everything is ok because of your religion. This is why Jesus told Nicodemus in John 3:5 that he had to be born again, otherwise he cannot see the kingdom of God. That is why today, the unity religion of Catholics, Muslims, Hindus and almost everyone else is taking over the world. However, we as Christians know that this is being perpetrated by the false prophet and the Anti-Christ. The second most common thing that keeps people out of the kingdom of God is sexual immorality. Even now, with the appearance of the saints, people are unwilling to give it up."

Pastor Tom then looked at me and asked me point blank,

"Have you and Diana had intimate relations yet?"

Diana turned red. I told the pastor quite honestly,

"No we did not but were tempted and in all honesty, I realize the importance of waiting until marriage."

I don't think he realized that. Pastor Tom then talked to us about our compatibility, love for each, if we liked each other as people and so on. Then he said,

"You should wait until you get married and if the temptation was too much we should live in separate places."

I explained to pastor Tom,

"Diana is both my spiritual mentor and my princess that I love her dearly and could not think of a finer woman to spend my life with."

Diana told pastor Tom,

"Bob is my strength in the flesh and my hero. I love his presence in a room, the confidence he has and how I feel whenever I am with him."

This of course only made me love her more. By this time, it was getting late and it was time to leave. When we left, our car was the only one left in the parking lot. I was so proud to have such a beautiful and spiritual woman as my wife to be. I grabbed her hand gently and placed it in mine as we walked to the car. Before I knew it 4 teenagers came out of nowhere and surrounded us. They started by saying things like,

"Hey pretty mama."

Then it got more vulgar, then they started talking about what would do to her after they ripped her clothes off. That was about all I could take. I explained to them,

"You are either going to walk away right now or you will not be able to walk."

So, the first tough guy said,

"I am going to stick you like a pig."

And pulled out a knife and came at me with it. I sidestepped the attack; wrist locked him, took the knife and implanted it in his right shoulder. While he was screaming from the pain the other 3 came at me.

I yelled for Diana,

"Get in the car and lock the doors."

Which she was able to do. I hit the first of the three with a front kick to the groin that dropped him like a sack of potatoes; he was unable to get to his feet for ten minutes. The second attacker received a palm heel strike to his solar plexus. He dropped and could not breathe. The third guy did get to me, as we were wrestling around, I locked up his arm in an arm breaking technique and asked him,

"Do I have to break it or would you prefer to run away."

He made the smart choice of running away. I immediately got in the car and took Diana home. She was quite shaken. She could not believe what just happened. Then the questions began,

"How did you learn to fight like that, did you have to stab the guy with his own knife, do you think you did the right thing by hurting all those guys?"

I explained to her,

"First and foremost I would not let anyone hurt you as long as I can help it."

I then explained my background a bit more.

"I was a Suffolk County wrestling champion that finished second in the state. Losing the state finals by a penalty point to a guy whose uncle refereed the match; that was a match I could never win. Then I spent 5 years training in karate and jujitsu under Don Johnson in Nassau County. Don was a national Jujitsu champion; he is the owner of Best Fitness kick boxing in Bellmore, NY. Don was not only a great instructor but a friend. Don was a Christian too and went missing on September 11th."

Diana thanked me profusely, told me,

"I love you."

And asked to go to sleep. That's how the day ended.

CHAPTER 6
NEW YEAR'S EVE ATTACK 2028

Sunday December 31, 2028 – New Year's Eve

I went to Sam's sporting goods and purchased a 20-gauge shotgun and a 22 rifle. After the incident last week, I told Diana,

"We have to have protection."

Diana doesn't like guns which I can understand. However, I told her,

"I love you too much to allow anyone to hurt you."

Since last week, Diana and I have gotten much closer; she couldn't believe that I would risk my life fighting four guys to protect her. Truthfully, I enjoyed showing off my skills. After shopping, I got home and we got ready for the midnight church service.

When we arrived at church it was packed. I mean hundreds of people; a lot of new faces, coming for the first time. I found pastor Tom and asked him,

"Do you want me to bring my new guns into the building?"

Pastor Tom stated,

"The church has security and you should relax."

Diana and I went in to find a seat. The usher gave us a corner seat in the back. I sat down and listened to the man sitting next to me. He said,

"I was walking outside last night and looked up and saw this resurrected saint preaching repent and believe, give glory to God, the maker of heaven and earth."

After that he had to come to church tonight and find out what is going on. Then the service began. The choir got up and started the praise and worship service. You could feel the spirit of God, in the church. People were touched and I watched a woman fall to her knees and just wept. A guy in the front of the church just fell to the ground, and laid on the floor speaking in tongues (unknown languages). After 20 mins of praise and worship pastor Tom came to the podium to begin the service. After a few kind words of how the spirit of God had moved and people were touched he said,

"Please bow your head in prayer."

As I bowed my head and closed my eyes, I heard someone yell out, in a loud voice,

"Allah Akbar!"

I quickly opened my eyes to see a bloody nightmare unfolding. 4 rows in front of me a man pulled out a 6-inch knife and was stabbing people as he yelled Allah Akbar. The church security team grabbed him and took him to the ground. Then another man who was sitting up front pulled out a machete and tried to attack the pastor. He took that machete and almost cut the podium in half. I looked at Diana, hesitated a bit, and then said,

"I have to help, Stay here."

I ran towards him picked up a chair along the way and hit this guy from behind as hard as I could. He fell forward and he lost the machete. I hit him again while he was down, then I asked 2 other congregants,

"Stay on him and not let him up."

And a third person I asked,

"Secure the machete."

People were screaming all over the church, a third man, yelling Allah Akbar was stabbing people to the left of me. He had stabbed an elderly woman who was on the ground bleeding, 2 teenage girls and a teenage boy. When the teenage boy fell to the ground, I was staring into the eyes of this maniac. I knew I was next; I quickly picked up a bible from a chair and used it as a shield as he attacked. My timing was great; he planted the knife into the center of the bible. I could then side-step him and get behind him. I took my right hand and cupped it under his right arm and barred up his left arm then I threw him over my back, landing him on his head. He was out cold. (This was one of my favorite wrestling moves in High School).

Then the police arrived took the 3 men into custody and took statements from all the witnesses. Diana was shaken but okay. I think she thought something like this would one day happen at the church. For me it was a defining moment. I now realized what I want to do when I graduate with my master's degree. I want to be a Secret Service Special Agent.

Before the police were done interviewing everyone, pastor Tom got up in front of the church and announced,

"As of tomorrow the church will become a soup kitchen, preparing food for the homeless and less fortunate. Church services will no longer be held here."

I am sure this is something that was planned due to the Pope giving all non-unity churches till January 2nd or face dire consequences. When Diana and I got home we prayed together asking God why? Why? Then Diana got a scripture Matthew 24:9. Suddenly it all made sense. I kissed her goodnight and went to bed.

(Then they shall deliver you up to be afflicted, and shall kill you: and ye shall be hated of all nations for my name's sake.) These were the times we are living in.

Monday, New Year's Day January 1, 2029

This morning Diana and I got up and turned on the television to hear Pope Peter giving another speech to the world. He said,

"All churches, synagogues and mosques must fly the Unity flag. We must all come under the same umbrella so that we can have peace throughout the world. Any church synagogue or mosque that does not have the unity flag flying in front of their building by tomorrow will be purged with fire. I am asking all my subjects to destroy the haters, burn their buildings, so that we could have a Unity religion. After this year is over, there will be only one religion in this world. And just like I called down fire for all to see I am asking my followers all to burn churches, synagogues and mosques to the ground that do not submit to our one-world religion and rid the haters from among us."

After Diana and I saw this on TV we got sick to our stomachs. We couldn't believe the world would follow such a man. I took Diana for a quiet romantic dinner but the whole time we felt distracted by Pope Peter's words and what might happen tomorrow.

Tuesday January 2nd, 2029

I got up early and went over to see pastor Tom and what used to be the church. When I arrived, he was having his morning coffee. We sat down to talk and as we did, we could hear gunfire erupting outside the building. I quickly got up to see what the disturbance was and there I saw the same five guys that shot out the church windows a few days ago.

I told pastor Tom,

"Stay in the building."

And I went out to talk to them. They asked,

"Where is the unity church flag?"

I explained to them,

"We are no longer a church, we are now just a soup kitchen. As a matter of fact, we were just taking the church sign down and replacing it with the new soup kitchen sign."

They were nice enough to shoot up the church sign and they totally destroyed it. Nevertheless, they left without any more damage and warned us,

"If you preach about Jesus here, we will destroy the place."

I went back and met with pastor Tom who prayed for peace and wisdom and then I headed back home to Diana. I was so tired from the day's events that after discussing with her what happened I had to go to bed.

Wednesday, January 3rd, 2029 - 8:00am

Pastor Tom called and said,

"Turn on your television!"

The world news network UVC was showing video of chaos throughout the world as the Unity church members on the Pope's command were burning all non-Unity places of worship and killing all non-Unity believers. To our horror we watched mass beheadings in Morocco, church members being burned alive in Spain. In Afghanistan hundreds of people were lined up and being shot dead. And here in the United States of America, acts of terror were taking place against Christians and Jews throughout the country. A Synagogue was blown up in Brooklyn, a Mormon church burned to the ground in Utah and chaos ruled the nation. At the end of the day Diana and I wept and prayed before we went to bed knowing that we are truly living in the tribulation period.

CHAPTER 7
THE NEW PRESIDENT TAKES OFFICE

Monday January 22nd 2029

Hillary Harris gets sworn in as the 48th president of the United States of America. With a democratic controlled house and Senate, she can do whatever she wants. The USA is now a one-party country. The Republicans have no power to stop anything. In her acceptance speech she talks about taxing the rich and climate change. She then signs an executive order forbidding the use of coal in any government buildings. Her plan is to raise taxes to 90% on the wealthy and give free healthcare and college tuition to all.

The most interesting thing to watch was how she thanked the "freedom from God foundation" for their support during the campaign.

Friday January 26th 2029

Congress passes a bill that will outlaw the Bible in all public schools. Congressman Cynthia Rogers stated,

"The bible is racist and sexist and exposing our young children to this garbage can cause children long term psychological damage. In defense of our children, I call upon all congressman to sign onto the bill and make it law."

It passed the house 250-185. A true sign that we live in terrible times.

Sunday- February 11th 2029

The Assyrian president today asked all former leaders of Muslim countries to submit to his authority as the Caliphate. He has given the Middle Eastern countries six months to comply. The countries of Morocco, Algeria, and Tunisia he has given 30 days. His worldwide Televised speech of unity under his worldwide authority was compelling. People throughout the Mideast could be seen cheering him on as he spoke. People seem to love this man.

Monday February 12, 2029

Diana and I went back to school today to begin our last semester before receiving our graduate degrees. I noticed a darkness over the campus and sensed an evil presence in my statistics class. My instructor had a strange glaze in her eyes; she seems to be demon possessed. All of a sudden and without warning she starts yelling,

"The haters are destroying the country because they won't join the unity religion. All Unity church members get an extra 20 points added to the grade point average for the semester."

I guess I am in trouble! Everything has changed. Things are so different since half the church was taken.

Friday February 16th, 2029

Today the US Senate passed the ban the Bible legislation by a 62-38 vote. It now moves to the desk of the president, Hillary Harris. President Harris plans to sign the legislation next Friday in the Rose Garden. They plan a big reception after the legislation is signed. The legislation will outlaw the bible in schools, and make possession of a bible a hate crime.

"The Freedom from Religion Foundation" held a parade in DC to honor the president for her support in banning the bible.

At that parade people were yelling and screaming praises for the Assyrian President. Here in America!

Tuesday February 20th 2029

As I was rushing to get to my 10am class I noticed a large crowd outside of the Business administration building. At least 100 students had gathered around and I could hear yelling and cursing but I couldn't see who they were yelling at. Soon students began to pick up rocks and sticks and were throwing them at the person that they had surrounded. Others were yelling Allah Akbar and saying that the Assyrian president would be their savior. Suddenly and without warning the person in the middle of this angry crowd levitated himself 10 feet in the air so all could see him. It was a resurrected saint that was there proclaiming the gospel of Jesus Christ. I was stunned to see the violent reaction to this supernatural being. His final words were,

"Jesus loves you. Repent and Believe."

And departed into the clouds. I was stunned and could not believe what I just had seen. I was 20 mins late for class. The hatred towards God was astounding, people who seem so nice turn so hateful and angry when God is mentioned. The gospel seems to trigger those people who are demon possessed, and more people seemed to be so than ever before!

Friday February 23, 2029

Big party in Washington as President Harris signs the bible ban into law. A parade was held with several thousand people marching against "Hate" now that they have banned the bible. Gays and homosexuals don't have to feel guilty about their behavior and no religious bigot can tell them that their behavior is wrong or offensive. The massive parade and after-party lasted well into the night. It was truly amazing to see the number of people that turned out to drink, party and mock the god of the bible. Every Hotel room in Washington was sold out for 3 straight nights!

Thursday March 1st, 2029

Today after moving his warships into the waters off of Morocco the Assyrian president ordered the attack on the country from five different points in a manner reminiscent of the World War II blitzkrieg. Within 72 hours the King of Morocco surrendered. The king agreed to become a client state and support the European Common Market nations. Diana and I noticed the jump in gas and food prices because of all these wars. Gas is now at $22.00 a gallon. I can't even fill up the car for $200 and I have a hybrid. Very hard to make ends meet. The cost of living is out of control.

The news media is all for the Assyrian president bringing forth a global unity and a one world religion. The media is also floating a new world order where America is controlled by the Assyrian President!

CHAPTER 8
GRADUATION DAY

Sunday May 6th, 2029

Diana and I are getting ready to graduate in a couple of weeks. I submitted my application to the United States Secret Service. Diana decided she wanted to teach. She is considering applying to teach at the community college once she graduates. On my way home I stopped for gas, I gave the cashier a $100.00 bill. After I put the $100 of gasoline into the gas tank I started the car and all it bought me was a half a tank of gas, crazy. But what makes matters worse is all the people hanging out at the gas station begging for $10 so they can put gas in their car, people simply can't afford to buy enough gas to go to work and live!

Monday May 28th, 2029

Today was graduation day. We both graduated with honors. I was so proud of her. Without her help I would not have had half as many A's. As we stood out on the lawn to receive our diplomas we saw a raptured saint. He came about ten feet above us and with a loud voice said,

"Repent and give glory to God, the maker of Heaven and Earth!"

All the attendees looked on in amazement. When we got home from graduation, we wondered what could happen next. We were already noticing that inflation is getting out of control. And certain commodities are becoming scarcer and scarcer.

I grabbed her hand to pray asking God for help to live through this terrible time. Diana and I then went shopping for fruit, vegetables, bread, eggs, milk and a few can goods. $106.00, these prices are just nuts!

When I arrived home Diana was watching Television. She said,

"Bob come here and watch this."

So I went over to the TV and watched as 5,000 people marched in New York City for free food and Rent! Mayor Mandammi promised $200 food vouchers for all to be used at city owned grocery stores. The problem is that there is little food at those stores. So the mayor had to address the crowd and calm the people. He said,

"The city will give publicly owned grocery stores $200 in cash for accepting the city vouchers and promised the people that the vouchers will be available by next Tuesday at all city DMV's and Police precincts."

This seemed to calm the people. Then he went on to say,

"The rent control freezes will stay in effect for another year."

Truly we are witnessing the collapse of civilization as we know it. People are getting to the point that they can't eat and keep a roof over their head. It seems like things will only get worse as time goes on.

Monday June 11th, 2029

Today the President of Assyria announced a new economic system. As of January 1st 2030, every man, woman, and child will have to receive a chip either on their hand or on their forehead to buy or sell anything in his kingdom. He said,

"This will cut government cost considerably, as a way of curtailing tax evasion, identity theft and will greatly increase the ability for the police to catch criminals and thwart kidnappings. This will demonstrate the unity among all my people to bring forth a one world religion and a one world government. All those that refuse to receive the chip will be exiled from the kingdom, or not be able to buy or sell."

As of March 3rd 2030, all currency will be illegal in the countries the President of Assyria (Caliphate) controls. He fully expects all his citizens to worship him like the Nazi's saluted Hitler.

As Diana and I sat watching this unfold on television I asked her,

"What do you think?"

Diana turned to me and said,

"Bob, this is what the Bible talks about in Revelation 13...that no man will buy or sell without the mark of the Beast."

So there we are watching Bible prophecy come to pass on television. And I asked Diana,

"What else can we expect."

She said,

"You can expect a lot more wars...You could expect the president of Assyria to attack Africa, the mid-East, South America and ultimately Israel."

Well, with that I was totally depressed and went to bed.

Thursday June 14, 2029

Diana and I are becoming closer and closer. We are totally in love with God and each other; we make an amazing couple. I also got the news that the Secret Service wants to interview me on July 9th. We went out to dinner to celebrate. While we were at the restaurant there were televisions playing at the sports bar. In the middle of dinner there was a breaking news story that the president of Assyria attacked Saudi Arabia and the United Arab Emirates. The news said that people loyal to the Assyrian president were sabotaging oil wells throughout Saudi Arabia. The news showed hundreds of oil wells on fire throughout the Saudi Arabian kingdom. Diana and I looked at each other and realized gas would probably jump to $25 a gallon. We decided to leave the restaurant then and go fill up our gas tanks already anticipating long lines at the pumps. We then purchased 7 five-gallon gas cans and filled those up too. You can't be too prepared these days.

Tuesday, June 26th, 2029

Today the king of Saudi Arabia announced his allegiance to the Assyrian President. Order was restored in the kingdom and they reallocated all available man power to putting out the fires in the oil wells that were destroyed. After the king of Saudi Arabia announced his submission to the Assyrian president; he asked other leaders in the mid-east, Yemen, Oman, Iraq, Jordan, Turkey, to also pledge their allegiance to him. Slowly but surely his kingdom is expanding and his arrogance is growing!

Statues are being placed in every country that he takes over, hundreds of them! With the help of AI, they seem to come to life and speak, telling all to worship him and cursing the God of the bible.

Monday, July 9th, 2029

Today was my interview with the United States Secret Service. It went very well. They have a lot of openings. It seems a lot of Secret Service agents went missing on Sept 11th, 2028. They asked me,

"How early can you start?"

I told them,

"September 9th to give me a little break from school before starting work and plan for the wedding and honeymoon."

I am planning to propose in the coming days. They gave me a whole bunch of forms to fill out and gave me a physical and made me take a lie detector test. They scheduled me for the secret service exam for Monday August 3rd. The secret service agent that I spoke with explained to me,

"They were hiring additional people because of the uprising in this country in support of the Assyrian president. A large number of Unity believers think the United States of America should submit to the European Common market and be subject to Sharia Law and the Assyrian President."

CHAPTER 9
THE SECRET SERVICE

Friday, July 20th, 2029

Diana and I went out to dinner and I proposed. I told her,

"I love you and want you to be my wife. With all that has happened this year, the attacks on the churches, the chaos on the streets, the $25 gas prices and inflation in food and rent. I think now more than ever it is important that we get married. I want you with me when I travel. I need you to pray with me every night. I need your love and spiritual guidance."

She happily agreed. We set August 31st of this year as our wedding date, just a small, simple ceremony with our closest friends and family. We took the time to pray about it and we felt the power of the Holy Spirit come upon us. More and more I feel the need to pray, I can't get through the day without the strength the holy spirit gives me. Overall, it was a very nice day.

Monday, July 30th, 2029

Today was a crazy day. Raptured saints were appearing to multitudes of people all over the country. Sightings were being reported all over the internet. Today differed greatly from any of the sightings beforehand. As Diana and I walked to the store, a Raptured Saint that she knew from church walked up to us and said,

"Be strong in the Lord and the Power of His might! He called you to be as one. I will use you to minister the gospel to kings and priests all over the world. One day you will be like me...immortal."

He then ascended into Heaven before our eyes and we were utterly amazed. The saint was dressed in a white robe and looked to be 25 years of age, with a glow around him.

Thursday, August 2, 2029

Today I sat for the Secret Service Exam. I studied hard and I felt I did really well. It was a two-hour long test. I left the office with a feeling of euphoria knowing that I aced that exam. When I got home, Diana was crying. She had the TV on and thousands of people were killed in an earthquake in California and she believed that her cousin was one of them because they were unable to reach her for the last five hours. The earthquake was 9.1 out of 10 on the Richter scale. It destroyed most of Los Angeles and Long Beach; CA. Diana said,

"This was another Biblical sign that we are in the end times."

Because of the earthquake, the President called out the National Guard. Hundreds of underground churches sent food and supplies to the victims.

Tuesday, August 7th, 2029

Another earthquake, stronger than the one in California hit Brazil today. It virtually destroyed Rio de Janeiro. Over 10,000 people have died and many more injured. We watched the devastation on Television and prayed before we went to bed.

Friday, August 17th, 2029

The president of Assyria sent the navy of the European Common Market Nations as well as ten ships from the Moroccan Navy to attack and invade

Brazil. With the Brazilian military trying to deal with the destruction of the earthquake they were quickly overrun by this Armada of ships and men that invaded the country. Within 48 hours Brazil agreed to submit to the authority of the president of Assyria. It seems to me that no nation can stand against him or his armies. In less than one year he has taken over the European Common Market nations, Morocco, Saudi Arabia, Iraq and the United Arab Emirates and now Brazil. I said to Diana,

"Who will stop him?"

She said,

"Bob, only the Lord himself."

She opened the Bible and showed me Revelation 19 where Christ will come to rule and reign. At that moment I felt a peace and a calm come over my soul that I could not explain. I could finally sleep soundly for the first time in months.

Saturday, August 18th 2029

I turned on the television this morning and there was the Assyrian president speaking against the God of Heaven. He said,

"Since I have taken over this body I have conquered many nations. The European Common Market nations are mine; Brazil is mine; Morocco is mine. I will come against all those haters that were taken out of the world that proclaim the Gospel of Jesus Christ. I will destroy Christians where ever they can be found. The so-called God of Heaven has no chance against me and I will destroy his servants where ever they might be. I ask my followers to rise up to kill these infidels where ever you can find them."

After hearing these words, I was sick to my stomach, turned off the television, and went to bed. But before Diana and I fell asleep we prayed for God's protection on our lives.

Saturday, September 1st, 2029

Today Diana and I got married. Pastor Tom officiated. It was a beautiful and heartwarming ceremony. We kept the ceremony really small. The food was great and everything was wonderful. We leave for Cancun tomorrow for a week. We are trying to keep things as normal as possible so we do not draw attention to ourselves. I start with the secret service the Monday following our return from Mexico. I feel so blessed to have Diana in my life. We had 50 people at the wedding and it cost us $30,000. Thank God, we got it back in gifts.

Monday, September 10th, 2029

Diana and I had an amazing honeymoon. We relaxed and had great food and a great time. Today was my first day at work and they assigned me to Beltsville, Maryland for training. Diana is going with me as we do not want to be apart during these perilous times. Training begins in a week. Today I spent it meeting the other agents in the office and learning my way around. I also met my new boss, Larry Lighthouse; his father adopted that last name because Larry's Grandfather was a Lighthouse keeper as was his great grandfather. Larry is my new boss. Larry singled me out and asked me into his office. He told me,

"I think you could be a great agent."

He had my file on his desk and asked me about my wrestling career, my wife and reviewed my college transcript with me. Overall, a great day at work, LL is the SSA (Supervisory Special Agent in the New York Field Office).

Tuesday, September 11th, 2029

Today is the One-year anniversary of the Rapture. A year ago today, everything started. The Rapture took the saints of God and it has been Hell ever since. We used to celebrate 9/11 as a memorial to the fallen victims of the terror attack on the Twin towers. Now instead hundreds of people are attending parades in many cities to honor the fact that the haters are gone and the Unity church has arrived. The pope gave a glorious speech over the progress he has made over the last year. The pope spoke about his determination to bring all countries and religions together under the leadership of the Assyrian president. He called fire down from Heaven again, spoke life into the statue of the Beast and announced that more countries would fall to the new one world order. With that his speech was interrupted by breaking news that the Assyrian president attacked Algeria and Tunisia earlier today. A 500,000-man army invaded from Morocco and 200 warships stormed the coast of the two countries thus forcing the Algerian army to pull back to the city of Adrar. Tunisia was so overwhelmed that it was forced to surrender. While this was taking place the God of Heaven released the raptured saints to descend upon the earth and preach the Gospel of Jesus Christ saying,

"Give Glory to God who made Heaven and earth. The Assyrian president cannot grant you eternal life...only Jesus Christ can."

Millions saw and heard the raptured saints marking the one-year anniversary of the Rapture. These are the times that the book of Revelation spoke about.

Monday, October 15th, 2029

Training is going well, and the bond between Diana and I is ever stronger. I love her so much and I am so grateful that she is here with me in these trying times. The U.S.A. is truly in a state of chaos. The followers of the Assyrian president continue to cause untold destruction. Backpack bombs are being exploded on buses, and shootings in malls and schools are common place. Any church that has tried to stay open aside from the Unity church is being targeted. In the 13 months that have passed since 9/11/2028 the price for our food and services has nearly doubled. While the murder rate has tripled, things just seem to get worse and worse. My boss Larry Lighthouse, LL for short, has big plans for me. LL wants me to try out for the elite Protection detail, where you protect high-risk dignitaries. I love the guy; he's a great boss so I agreed to do it.

Thanksgiving, Thursday, November 29th, 2029

We made a special effort to remain thankful for all that we have even in these desperate times. We went home to see everyone and had dinner at Pastor Tom's house.

The church building can no longer be used as a church; it had to be turned into a soup kitchen to avoid vandalism and other issues. As a result, the believers in Christ must meet at private residences to avoid problems.

After we prayed, we turned on the TV to watch football, but instead of seeing the game the news interrupted us. We watched in horror as the president of Assyria beheaded 5000 people on the shores of Tripoli. They captured these Christians from Tunisia and Algeria who refused to bow down to him. He brought these men, women and children to the beach where they brought forth 100 people at a time to be beheaded at the shore. Their blood turned the sea red. The heads were collected and the bodies were left for the blood to drain into the sea. Afterwards, they buried the bodies in a mass grave. Another sad day in the history of this world, even our own president is afraid to engage him. The Assyrian President seems to have the entire world in fear of him; it's like watching Hitler on steroids.

Christmas Day, Tuesday, December 25th, 2029

The Assyrian president declared this day a day of praise and worship to him alone. He said,

"Who is this Jesus? Can he conquer as I conquer? Is he feared like I am feared? To prove my power and might I have set my armada to take The Philippines and Brunei."

712 ships amassed around these two nations. The Philippines navy of 55 vessels was set out to defend the country. Those 55 ships were destroyed within hours. And the Assyrian president proclaimed,

"I alone am the god of this world and no one can stand against me."

What can be done? Again, even the United States stood by and did nothing.

CHAPTER 10
NEW YEAR'S DAY 2030

THE ANTI-CHRIST BEGINS TO EXPAND HIS TERRITORY

New Year's Day 2030

What a day, half the world is controlled by the Assyrian president and here in America his support is growing by leaps and bounds. Another parade to celebrate his victory overseas. Now they put a statue that talks with the use of AI in Times Square in New York. People go there and pray to it daily. I am astonished at the hatred these worshippers have towards Christians and Jews.

A group of Christians went to Times Square to pray for people and preach the gospel and within an hour they were surrounded by a gang of illegal migrants and beaten. The police responded and stopped it before it got too out of hand. However, the Christians were all given tickets, which have a $1,000 fine for preaching the gospel and causing a commotion. The gang got away without consequence.

Amazing how things can change so quickly, two years ago the gang members would have gone to jail. I am glad that I will be carrying a gun and have the ability to defend myself and others!!

Monday, March 4th, 2030

I completed my Secret Service training and was assigned to the New York field office, as I expected; LL made sure that I would be working for him. It is good to have a guardian angel at work. I got my first case today. The chaos in the world overshadowed my happy day at work.

The Assyrian president announced plans to expand his kingdom into Africa. He has sent delegations to Angola, Congo, Nigeria, Cameroon, and Namibia. He is giving these countries 60 days to submit to his Kingship.

He announced that if these countries do not voluntarily submit to him, he will behead all those that do not comply.

Tuesday, July 16th, 2030

Today Angola and the Congo announced that they would resist the Kingship of the Assyrian president. But Nigeria, Cameroon, and Namibia willingly submitted to him. As a result, the president of Assyria announced within the next few months he will destroy Angola and the Congo.

Inflation is raging around the world as these never-ending wars continue. Every new nation that is taken over must submit to the chip payment system. No one can buy or sell without a chip implanted in your hand or forehead. It's impossible to enter a store unless you have the chip. God help us all!!!

CHAPTER 11
ASSIGNED TO MEET THE ANTICHRIST

Wednesday, September 11th, 2030

Today they assigned me the Secret Service protection detail of the Assyrian president for his upcoming visit. LL thought such an assignment would help my career, and he knew that I would do a great job!! The Assyrian President will arrive here on Tuesday, September 17th to work out a peaceful negotiation between Angola and the Congo.

It is the 2nd anniversary of the rapture. The Unity Church had parades all over the country to celebrate the taking of the haters. They even put the parade on television like it was the Macy's parade. I watched in disbelief as the Pope spoke of the progress that the world has made over the last 2 years.

They had gay pride floats as well as floats for the Assyrian President and the Unity Church to top it off they set up 6 AI statues along the parade route that seemed to come alive and speak to people as they passed by.

Pope Peter told all the people there to enjoy the day and worship the one true conqueror the Assyrian President himself. I got sick to my stomach and turned the TV off.

Monday, September 16th, 2030

Today I left for Manhattan to get my hotel room at the Grand Region Hotel where the President of Assyria will be staying. As I walked to the hotel, I could see the pride flags and parade material littering the streets from the parade a few days before. The hotels just started to empty out today from all the visitors that came to see the parade.

What a bunch of freaky people can be seen on the streets of Manhattan. I saw more people with blue hair and tattoos then I saw blondes. More nose rings and piercings than normal looking upstanding citizens.

We had a meeting of all the Secret Service agents assigned to this detail. Thank God the Secret Service still has a high bar of quality individuals. They understand the need to hire capable people who can protect and serve. The Agents of the Secret Service love their job and are committed to Excellence in all they do, I am truly blessed to work for such a great organization.

They assigned me to pick up the Assyrian president at the airport. I was a little apprehensive about meeting him, I think he is the devil in disguise but so many people love him. I can't help but wonder what it will be like to be in his presence. I am a bit curious. It will be a very interesting detail. I am one of 6 Agents assigned to guard him, some of the Agents have been around for 20 years. Our detail will supplement his personal bodyguards from Assyria. Each dignitary must get a Secret Service detail when they come into the USA.

Some of the older agents have worked with him before and said that his people are OK to work with, which put me at ease.

Tuesday, September 17th, 2030

I and four other agents left the hotel for Kennedy airport where we were to meet the president of Assyria. At 10:30am his plane arrived. We drove him and his delegation back to the hotel. He rode in my car. We did not make eye contact. He was talking to one of his security personnel the entire time we drove to the hotel.

We arrived at the hotel and went up through the service entrance. When we got to the room the DOD just finished its bomb sweep. At that point in time, I had the opportunity to shake his hand and welcome him to the United States of America.

He has a towering presence. He was at least 10 inches taller than I am and has fierceness in his eyes that I have never seen in any other man. His security detail is very astute with many capable men. Each and every one of them is built like a bodybuilder with eyes as sharp as eagles and menacing to behold. As I watched them, I prayed I would never have to engage any of them at any point in time. Although I am skilled, these men frighten me.

The president of Assyria stated he would like to go to Spark's Steakhouse for dinner and we made the necessary arrangements sending an advance team to secure the establishment. Two hours later we picked him up at his room, got in the motorcade and proceeded to Spark's Steakhouse.

When we arrived and entered the restaurant, to my great surprise people were falling down to worship him. One old man that recognized him, fell to his knees and said,

"Great anointed one, I have waited my whole life to see you. Now I can die in peace."

We had to ask the restaurant owner to put us in a separate room away from the public because he was more popular than I ever imagined. His detail leader told me that this happens everywhere that he goes. As a result, they carry special scanners that can detect a firearm or knife on a person. The scanners make it easier for them to protect him.

I was sitting within hearing distance of him all throughout dinner. Right before the main meal was served one of the president's Generals arrived to join him for dinner. As the meal was served, they began to talk. The General told the president that the requested 550 ship Armada would be ready by March 1, 2031. To my surprise they started talking about military tactics.

The president instructed the General to have 8 aircraft carriers in the South China Sea by March 1st also. Five were to be placed South of Malaysia and Indonesia, the other 3, outside of the waters of the Federated States of Micronesia. He explained to the General that first he needed to sign a peace treaty with Australia. Then they will begin to move the Armada into place.

He told the General that he is meeting the Prime Minister of Australia on November 22nd and he would have the treaty signed then. Then he boldly told the General that the people of Malaysia and Indonesia are his people and he will have them.

As I listened, I could hear him tell his General how they would blockade the countries with the Armada and stop all oil tankers going into the countries. If they did not surrender within 90 days they would invade, knowing that they would have no gas to power their vehicles and ships. Sounded like a brilliant plan.

Then to my surprise LL showed up. He came over to me asked me how I was doing. I told him great. Then I watched as he stepped out of the room with the Assyrian President. I could still see him in the other room as he kissed the ring of the Assyrian president and bowed to him. I felt myself get nauseous. I couldn't believe it, my boss, a man I love and appreciate bowing down to the evilest man alive. How am I going to tell Diana?

The dinner ended and we took him back to the hotel without incident, but I was sick to my stomach knowing my boss worships the President of Assyria.

Wednesday, September 18th, 2030

I was assigned to guard the hotel room door of the president of Assyria. At 1:00 pm he left his room to meet with the presidents of Congo and Angola. When he left, the Secret Service detail leader reassigned me to the meeting room where the president of Assyria was meeting with the other two presidents.

When we went into the meeting room, I was standing next to the president of Assyria looking at the presidents of Congo and Angola. I could see the fear in their eyes. They looked like frightened children and then they sat down and he began to speak. The president of Assyria said,

"Have you not seen what I have done to the other countries that have come against me? How I have destroyed them? Submit to me and I will allow you to stay in the position of president as a client state. You will pay a tax to my kingdom but I will not kill your people nor destroy your nation. Your people will acknowledge me as God of this world. They will have no gods before me. If you do this you will live. If not, my armies will destroy your nation and you, your wife and your children will be beheaded in front of me. You have 24 hours to make your decision. The choice is yours."

After the meeting we left the room and I took the president of Assyria back to his hotel room. Truly his presence is fierce, menacing and frightening. He instills fear in all who meet him. God help this world.

Thursday, September 19th, 2030

Today I was again assigned to the meeting room of the President of Assyria, Congo, and Angola. The president of the Congo agreed to his terms as did the president of Angola. The Assyrian president now controls six African countries, as well as Europe, The Philippines, Brunei, and a good part of the Middle East.

He informed the presidents of Angola and the Congo that he will be taking control of their armies to take control of more of Africa. When the meeting was over the Assyrian president went to his room, packed and headed for the airport. I stayed at the hotel room until such time as the flight went wheels up (airborne). Then I headed home to see Diana.

Saturday, September 21st, 2030

Today I was home with Diana enjoying my day off. I was relaxing on the couch watching Diana vacuum the living room, when she was done, she turned on the television. She inadvertently turned on the news. The Assyrian president that I just met was giving a news conference. He was telling the world that all citizens in all the territories he controls must receive a mark on their head or their hand or they won't buy or sell.

The Assyrian President announced that all cash will be worthless as of January 31st, 2031. All citizens must take their cash to the bank before that to get credit for it. He announces that every post office, library, and school will be implanting chips in people Monday – Friday from 9am-8pm beginning Monday morning until the last day of January.

I sat there in disbelief and Diana said,

"This is exactly what the Bible said would happen."

Sure enough, this man has taken over half the world and now people won't be able to buy or sell unless they have his mark of allegiance implanted in them. Come quick Lord Jesus.

Saturday, November 30th, 2030

Today it was announced that the President of Assyria signed a peace treaty with Australia. One of my Secret Service friends told me that he was protecting the president of Australia last week and had the chance to hear him talking to his security people.

He told me that they are petrified of the Assyrian president and will adopt the right to bear arms into their constitution next week so that people will have the ability to protect themselves in the event of a breach in the peace treaty. It is truly amazing to see the fear that this one man can cause the world.

CHAPTER 12
CHRISTMAS 2030 - A DAY TO REMEMBER

Wednesday, December 25th, 2030

Christmas Day - I was home with Diana exchanging gifts when the phone rang. It was 3pm and Diana and I were enjoying a nice day by the fireplace getting cozy. I answered the phone and it was LL, the Russians and the Chinese decided to come to the UN to meet in Manhattan. They were shorthanded and I am the new kid on the block so I got selected for the protection detail. I have to be at the Waldorf Astoria Hotel tomorrow for a 5-day assignment. I have to protect President Chi of China.

As fate would have it Diana was super excited about the gift that she got me. She was uncontrollable jumping up and down as she gave it to me. All she could say was open it, open it!! Well, I finally opened it and what a great gift it is. She gave me an earpiece that translates 175 languages. Diana said,

"Now you can listen to the Russians when they speak to the Chinese, and no one will know."

I immediately set up the device and sure enough I put on the television and went to the Spanish speaking channel and it worked like a charm!! I then had to pack and get ready for the trip. I am now prepared for tomorrow's detail.

CHAPTER 13
PROTECTING CHINA & RUSSIA

Thursday, December 26th, 2030

I arrived at the Waldorf Astoria Hotel at 10am. I checked into my room and found the Command Center on the 2nd floor of the hotel. Special Agent Robert Vilardi was the detail leader. I would be working 8am to 8pm shifts for the 5 days that I will be here. Rob has been with the Secret Service for 10 years and I have worked with him before, we have a good rapport and he always treats me well.

Today I will be standing post outside President Chi's hotel room until 8pm. Our intel has his flight landing at JFK at 7pm, so a good chance I won't see him today.

I stayed in the command center drinking coffee and talking with the other agents until DOD (Dept. of Defense) arrived with the bomb sniffing dog. Then I took them up to the 5th floor where the President of China would be staying. I watched and waited as they swept the room for explosives. There were 2 agents and 1 dog. They were talking about how China and Russia want to partner to stop the Assyrian President from taking over any more countries. I listened intently as they spoke. They are coming here to quietly put together a plan. The next few days will be interesting. My Christmas gift (the language translator) will certainly come in handy. I can't wait to listen to what they have to say.

After the room was swept, I stood post until 8pm. At this point President Chi was on the way to the hotel but stuck in traffic, I will meet him tomorrow. After being relieved from my post I went to my room and unpacked and took a shower. I ate a little something and went to bed.

Friday, December 27th, 2030

I got up at 6:30 am to shower and dress. I arrived at the Command post at 7:30am had a cup of coffee and a bagel. The Secret Service does a good job providing for their agents. At 5 minutes to 8am I went to the President's room and relieved the other Agent and took the post outside of President Chi's room. Things were quiet until noon, that's when site leader Vilardi showed up. He said that President Yeltsin of Russia was on the way. (President Putin of Russia died back in 2027 of a heart attack and Yeltsin, the grandson of the former leader of Russia took his place with a resounding election victory.)

Vilardi told me that he wanted me inside the room as additional security and another agent would be up to take my place in 5 minutes. A few minutes later up comes my replacement and I knock on the door of President Chi's room and his security opens the door and site leader Vilardi explains to his security that the Secret Service would like an additional Agent in the room as a precaution. After a 3-minute discussion they agreed.

I was asked to stand by the window in the living room. The 2 Presidents plan to speak in the living room when President Yeltsin arrives. A few minutes passed before President Chi emerged from the bedroom wearing a black suit and red tie. When he saw me standing in the living room, he asked his security who I was in Chinese, and to my surprise I understood everything he said through my translator in my ear. However, I was careful to keep this a secret. His security explained to him that the Secret Service wanted another agent in the room. He was fine with it and said hello to me in English. He then asked if I wanted coffee or a blueberry muffin. I thanked him for the gesture but politely declined.

Then as a precautionary measure I went to the window took out my binoculars and scanned the outside building for any suspicious activity, like people on rooftops and saw none. Then the radio call came in that President Yeltsin was on his way to the room. ETA 7 minutes.

When President Yeltsin arrived, he greeted President Chi with a warm hug. It was apparent that these 2 men were friends. President Chi insisted that they have coffee and muffins, so they sat down at the dining room table and ate muffins and sipped coffee. The entire time making small talk asking each other about their families.

To my surprise the translator in my ear translated Chinese and Russian equally well.

When they finished eating the muffins and drinking the coffee it was time for the talks to begin. President Chi expressed his concern about the rapid expansion of terrorism since the Assyrian president has taken over. Over this short time, he has been in power. President Yeltsin shared his concern and emphasized the need for China and Russia to form an alliance that will discourage the Assyrian from attacking either of their nations.

President Yeltsin told President Chi that he had a detailed plan that he wanted to share with him. He said that his plan would change the world and neutralize the plans of the Assyrian leader. However, he could not go into detail today, since he promised his wife and children a shopping spree at Saks 5th Avenue. He just wanted to make sure that President Chi would have his back. President Chi stated that he hates the Assyrian and is committed to helping his friend President Yeltsin.

President Chi said goodbye and President Yeltsin left for his shopping spree. President Chi stated that he was tired and went to take a nap.

I notified the shift leader that the meeting was over and he told me to go eat, take an hour for lunch and meet back at the command post. I found a nice Chinese Restaurant on 2nd Avenue and 53rd street and enjoyed a nice meal. An hour later I was back in the command center. Shift leader Vilardi told me that I wasn't needed until tomorrow so I called it a day a bit early.

Saturday, December 28th, 2030

Got up at 6:30am and out the door by 7:30am, arriving at the command center at 7:43 am. I grabbed a coffee and a donut. Shift leader Vilardi stated that he wanted me in the room again today. So, I went upstairs to President Chi's room to wait for the meeting with President Yeltsin to start.

At 10am President Yeltsin showed up with 4 extra people. He told President Chi that he had charts and graphs to show him and asked if he could have them set up in the living room. President Chi agreed and the 4 men went to work. After ten minutes the living room was filled with charts and graphs. President Yeltsin asked President Chi to sit down so he could begin to explain what his plans were.

Being in the room with them and having a translator in my ear made it easy to both hear and understand everything that they were saying.

President Yeltsin began the meeting by telling President Chi that since the Assyrian president has been taking over Europe and other countries, he has been having secret meetings with leaders from North Korea, Iran, Turkey, Yemen, UAE, and Saudi Arabia. President Yeltsin explained that the main focus of the Assyrian is to conquer Israel. So, Yeltsin explained that with the Chinese Army as back up, he could invade Israel take the country and control the World.

Yeltsin explained that the combined armies of Russia, Turkey, Iran, North Korea, Yemen, UAE, Libya, and Saudi Arabia will number over 3,000,000 men and will be unstoppable. Yeltsin also stated that he is still talking with Ethiopia and Ukraine for additional forces. Yeltsin told Chi that he is considering giving back Crimea if Ukraine gives him 200,000 men to invade Israel.

President Chi was impressed looking at the charts and graphs and seeing how the invasion would occur. Yeltsin explained that the takeover of Israel will give them weapons and technology necessary to defeat the Assyrian President in the event of a war. Yeltsin stated that he would share the weapons with China.

President Chi stated he would be willing to supply tanks and invasion vehicles at reasonable prices. Chi told Yeltsin that China could produce its newest tank for $5,000,000 apiece and could deliver 2,000 of them within 9 months. Yeltsin called an associate into the room to run this proposition by him. After a few questions back and forth Yeltsin said that Russia can make payments using natural gas and oil. Chi would agree as long as China received a minimum of 25,000 barrels of oil per tank, it could be more but never less depending on market conditions. Yeltsin said congratulations we have a deal.

President Chi then said let's go to Sparks Steakhouse to celebrate. At this point it was only 4pm but President Yeltsin said let's do it and plans were put in place for it to happen. Secret Service sent a lead agent there to make sure there would be no security risk. Yeltsin left for his room to get ready and Chi went into his bedroom to shower and dress for the dinner.

When Chi left for dinner, I stayed in the room until 8pm when my shift ended. I went back to my room and called Diana and told her what I heard but I only gave her limited snippets. When the detail is over, I will tell her everything. After we spoke, I grabbed a quick dinner and went to bed.

Sunday, December 29th, 2030

Another day, getting up at 6:30am and reporting to the command center by 7:30am. The shift leader stopped by to tell me that President Chi liked having me in the room. I was happy to hear it and I knew that he didn't know that I had a translator in my ear, if he did he probably wouldn't be talking so openly.

Today is my last day in the room, tomorrow President Chi leaves for China. It will be an eventful day. I arrived in the room at 7:55am and was greeted by the President's security. They invited me in and offered me coffee and a bagel with cream cheese. The head of Chi's security spoke English and told me that after eating dinner last night at Spark's Steakhouse the 2 presidents went to a private strip club. This club is actually approved by the UN for entertaining dignitaries from all over the world and the UN supplies security so no one has to worry. They didn't return until 5am so today's meeting won't start till 2pm.

We watched "It's a Wonderful Life" on television until 1:45 pm when President Chi emerged from the bedroom. He said good afternoon and asked his security advisor when President Yeltsin would be arriving. After a few calls were made word came back that Yeltsin would arrive at 2:20pm.

Sure enough at 2:21 there was a knock at the door - It was President Yeltsin and his security detail. The two presidents greeted each other and talked about the night before. How amazing the dinner was and the great time that they had at the club afterwards.

Both President Chi and President Yeltsin had translators so they could understand each other but none of their security detail did. No one knew that I had a translator and could understand everything that was being said. So, the presidents spoke freely and exposed all their plans!!!

President Yeltsin began the meeting by thanking President Chi for the tanks and stated that he is planning the invasion of Israel for September of next year. President Chi said that tank deliveries will start in March and will continue until all 2,000 tanks are delivered before September 1st of 2031.

President Yeltsin said that would be great so that his soldiers can practice with the tanks delivered in March and April and every month until the full allotment is delivered. Yeltsin then told Chi that he has a special tank shell that will be fired from their tanks.

This shell will be a bio weapon that will only kill people and not destroy buildings.

Yeltsin said that this is the key to winning the war. Yeltsin said,

"We can take all of Israel's nuclear weapons, the Iron Dome system and their advanced rifle systems and use them to destroy the Assyrian President and his forces."

President Yeltsin went on to explain that his scientist is developing a vaccine that will prevent his soldiers from getting the virus that will be exposed to all the Israeli people, once it is fired from the tanks. This virus will be 100x worse than COVID-19 and leave anyone who is exposed to it unable to walk or breathe. So unless someone is vaccinated, they won't be able to function. Right now, Yeltsin said that his scientists are months away from a vaccine that won't have side effects to the soldiers that take it.

Yeltsin told Chi that the world would be a better place if him and Chi controlled it and not the Assyrian President. President Yeltsin said this plan will work!! It will allow Israel to be fully controlled by Russia and its friends. President Chi offered the services of his labs throughout China to help speed up the vaccine.

Yeltsin said this must be kept secret, a total surprise for all the world to see, the final defeat of Israel and the Jewish people!!!

It was only 7pm when the meeting ended but President Yeltsin said he was still tired and had to fly back to Moscow tomorrow morning. The 2 Presidents parted with a hug and a handshake. The ball has been put in motion for Israel to be invaded!!!

I stayed till my 8pm shift was over, then went to dinner at a Chinese restaurant on 52nd and 2nd Avenue. They have amazing spicy chicken. Then it was back to the room and off to bed. Called Diana quickly to tell her that I loved her.

Monday, December 30th, 2030

Last day of the detail. Up at 6:30am at the command post at 7:30am. I got to the room before 8am. Security let me in and I had coffee and a bagel with the other members of President Chi's security team. By 9am President Chi was getting packed up to leave. He was moving luggage from the bedroom to the living room, when his phone rang. He answered and I could tell from the conversation it was President Yeltsin.

It seems that he forgot to ask President Chi for 1,000 medium range drones for the invasion. They agreed upon price and terms but I couldn't hear what they were. Sounds like this is going to be bigger than when Germany invaded Russia. President Yeltsin really believes that he can overtake the Assyrian President after he captures Israel.

By 11am President Chi was out the door heading to JFK to take his plane home. The shift leader called and told me to hold the room until President Chi's plane is in the air. At 3pm President Chi's plane went wheels up and I got the call to leave the room and go to the command center. Shift leader Vilardi came in and said check out of the hotel and go home. So I did.

I made it home for dinner. I was so excited to see Diana and couldn't wait to share with her all that happened during the detail. By 7pm I was so tired that I could no longer keep my eyes open and had to go right to sleep. I promised Diana that I would share all the details of the last few days tomorrow.

CHAPTER 14

NEW YEAR'S EVE - OUT WITH FRIENDS

Tuesday, December 31st, 2030

Today is New Year's Eve - I can't believe it - where does the time go. I was so tired from the protection detail that I didn't get up till 11am. Diana made me a nice breakfast and reminded me that we are going to a New Year's Eve dinner with our friends Brendan and Sandi McGuiness. They got dinner reservations at 9 pm at the Fountains Steakhouse in Bellmore, Long Island.

Brendan and Sandi are Christians too and much like us were not prepared for the Rapture when it happened. We have forged a tight relationship and are counting down the days to the end of the dispensation of grace, which is exactly 1260 days from the day of the rapture. Well 780 days has passed since that fateful event. Jesus said he who endures till the end shall be saved.

Every time we get together, we encourage each other to endure until the end. Brendan is always talking about Revelation 7:9 when there are so many people in heaven that no man can number and when John asks where these people came from, he is told that these are the people that came out of great tribulation. Brendan reminds us that these people will never again be hungry or thirsty and God will wipe every tear from their eyes.

We encourage each other and keep a calendar to help the stress of living in this nightmare of a world. Thankfully, working 12-hour shifts added a lot of overtime to my check, which gave me the money to pay for a nice dinner.

As we were waiting for our server, the cell phones started beeping - everyone's cell phone alerted at the same time!! A dictate from the Vatican was just released - Pope Peter is asking all Unity believers to kill anyone trying to make them believe in Jesus Christ. He said that people who still hold to the old belief that Jesus is Lord are fools that need to die. He said we can never move forward as long as people like this live!!

For the sake of one world religion and peace on earth please sacrifice these evil people that stand in our way!!

Needless to say, a chill ran through my spine as I read those words. It wouldn't be long before mobs were in the streets looking to obey the dictate of the Pope.

Sure enough, 5 minutes after we began to eat, we heard a commotion in the parking lot. We couldn't see what was happening but we could hear it. Someone was in the parking lot with a sign that said Jesus saves. Suddenly cars pulled into the parking lot, 4 or 5 of them - with people screaming kill the unbeliever!!

I wanted to go outside and see what was happening but before I could do it, a large man about 6 feet tall with a beer belly, red hair and a beard came running into the restaurant with a bat in his hands. He started yelling if there are any Christians here, I am here to kill you too. With that comment he looked at us and came over towards the table. Before he could get too close, I stood up and drew my gun. I said,

"Bob Klement United States Secret Service - these people are under my protection."

He looked at me, saw the gun pointed at him and said,

"I don't give a fuck, if they are Christians they must die."

As he said it, he began to foam at the mouth - it became obvious to everyone that this guy was demon possessed.

I then explained to him that the gun pointed at him was a 9mm with one round in the chamber and 13 more in the magazine and if that wasn't enough there were 3 more magazines with 13 rounds each. In the event that wasn't enough firepower I told him that I have a backup 45 with 8 rounds in it and an additional 7 round magazine.

That seemed to get him to stop in his tracks but at that moment 4 of his buddies came running into the restaurant all with bats, clubs or tire irons. This emboldened him and he said to his buddies,

"I bet they are Christians too."

That's when Brendan stood up - he is not a small man - he's over 6'4" tall with a muscular build. He was an amateur boxer that went the distance with Mike Tyson and Riddick Bowe. Needless to say, he is definitely a tough guy.

Brendan pulled out a 357 magnum and said,

"I think you boys are at the wrong restaurant, you need to leave. If you don't, I am going to start shooting, just so you know my gun has very special rounds in it. They are made of titanium and will blow your limbs off. So, if I shoot you in the leg, the bullet will separate your leg from your body, so what do you want to do. Do you want to go ahead and make my day or do you want to live another day."

At that moment Brendan pulls the hammer back on his 357 and smiled. The red headed guy said,

"Fuck you,"

and then turned around and left. It was a harrowing experience for us all.

Living in a world where everyone wants you dead and you must always be armed and ready. It was hard for us to finish dinner. We were thankful that we lived through the evening.

When we went to leave the restaurant there was an ambulance in the parking lot, the poor guy that was carrying the sign Jesus saves was beaten to death. They were putting a sheet over his body as we looked for our car. Before we could leave a police officer stopped us and asked if we saw anything and we said we were eating at the time of the commotion. He asked for ID and I showed him my Secret Service credentials and he called it in to verify it. He then returned and said we could leave. Not the New Year I expected.

CHAPTER 15
DIANA'S EXPLANATIONS

January 3rd, 2031

After 2 days of resting and praying it is time to sit down with Diana and tell her what I overheard at the meeting with President Chi and President Yeltsin. I started the conversation by saying that Russia is planning a massive invasion of Israel sometime in the fall. President Chi has agreed to supply drones and tanks. Russia is waiting for the equipment. Yeltsin has already amassed a vast army from many nations. He has gotten promises from both Iran and Turkey and numerous other mid-east countries. They believe that their coalition of countries can offset the power of the President of Assyria by invading and conquering Israel. Israel is the key to controlling the world as Yeltsin put it.

Diana said this is just what the Bible said would happen!!! I said where does it say that. She said in Ezekiel chapter 38.

"This is what the Sovereign Lord says: At that time evil thoughts will come to your mind, and you will devise a wicked scheme. You will say, 'Israel is an unprotected land filled with unwalled villages! I will march against her and destroy these people who live in such confidence! I will go to those formerly desolate cities that are now filled with people who have returned from exile in many nations. I will capture vast amounts of plunder, for the people are rich with livestock and other possessions now. They think the whole world revolves around them!' But Sheba and Dedan and the merchants of Tarshish will ask, 'Do you really think the armies you have gathered can rob them of silver and gold? Do you think you can drive away their livestock and seize their goods and carry off plunder?'

"Therefore, son of man, prophesy against Gog. Give him this message from the Sovereign Lord: When my people are living in peace in their land, then you will rouse yourself. You will come from your homeland in the distant north with your vast cavalry and your mighty army, and you will attack my people Israel, covering their land like a cloud. At that time in the distant future, I will bring you against my land as everyone watches, and my holiness will be displayed by what happens to you, Gog. Then all the nations will know that I am the Lord.

"This is what the Sovereign Lord asks: Are you the one I was talking about long ago, when I announced through Israel's prophets that in the future I would bring you against my people? But this is what the Sovereign Lord says: When Gog invades the land of Israel, my fury will boil over! In my jealousy and blazing anger, I promise a mighty shaking in the land of Israel on that day. All living things - the fish in the sea, the birds of the sky, the animals of the field, the small animals that scurry along the ground, and all the people on earth - will quake in terror at my presence. Mountains will be thrown down; cliffs will crumble; walls will fall to the earth. I will summon the sword against you on all the hills of Israel, says the Sovereign Lord. Your men will turn their swords against each other. I will punish you and your armies with disease and bloodshed; I will send torrential rain, hailstones, fire, and burning sulfur! In this way, I will show my greatness and holiness, and I will make myself known to all the nations of the world. Then they will know that I am the Lord."

Diana said that God is hardening the heart of Yeltsin just like he did to Pharaoh King of Egypt. God is doing this so that he can show the world his glory and power. It will be the last great miracle he does before the dispensation of grace ends.

Everyone throughout the world will see the devastation of the earthquake and the millions of dead soldiers who tried to invade Israel. This will be the event that brings many to salvation. No matter how powerful people think the President of Assyria is he can't destroy a million-man army in a few minutes like God can. So many that still haven't taken the Mark of the Beast will get saved.

CHAPTER 16
THE U.N. DETAIL

Larry told me that I will be working a 3-day detail that starts tomorrow at the UN. I will be protecting the President of Assyria again. After the detail ends to take Friday off because paying overtime is a problem, due to budget issues so in lieu of overtime I can take a day off.

There are 3 of us from our office assigned to the detail, I am working with Harry Heinz and Ted Williams. We met to discuss who will be doing what. We understand that he is coming to the UN to ask the UN general assembly to vote for a global monetary system. That system requires a chip be implanted into each person's hand or head. The Assyrian president has implemented this system in all nations he controls. Now he wants it to be worldwide because visitors to Europe and the Middle East can't buy or sell in the countries he controls. He wants the UN general assembly to ratify this system and make it law.

The three of us were in a conference room in the office discussing who would be doing what, when all of a sudden LL, our supervisor burst into the room with unexpected news. LL stated that 4,000,000 people will descend upon New York City tomorrow to support the Assyrian President's move for a one world economic system. He stated that it is mandatory that we carry our backup gun, which is a GAP 45 by Glock. With a total of 5 magazines for our normal FN 9MM. Additionally, our Spectra shield bulletproof vests and stun guns are required. NYPD will have 35,000 officers on duty 24/7 for all 3 days. This is going to be a crazy detail.

I went home to my amazing wife Diana and told her about the detail. Diana is both beautiful and smart, so as I spoke, she started to reference a verse in the Bible. In Revelation 13:16-17 says that He (the Assyrian President) will require everyone to take a mark on their hand or forehead. And no one could buy or sell anything without that mark, which was either the name of the beast or the number representing his name. Wisdom is needed here.

Diana went on to say that this detail will see the Assyrian president win the approval of the UN and change the world forever. Diana said the USA has become weak and President Harris, the first woman president is gravely fearful of the Assyrian President. Diana said that she will agree to his demands. The march on New York City is to show the world how much power he has. After that brief discussion I had to pack and get ready for the detail tomorrow.

CHAPTER 17
THE DARK BEGINNING

Harry, Ted, and I arrived at the UN building to assist with the protection of the Assyrian President. With millions of people in town to support his speech at the UN the traffic is crazy. I got assigned to guard the exit door inside the room where the Assyrian President would be speaking. I had my translator in my ear so that I could understand every word that is spoken.

Reports were coming over the radio about the crowd sizes outside. Millions of people from all over the country flooded the streets of Manhattan. It was so bad that the Assyrian President was forced to park his car 6 blocks away and walk on foot. NYPD sent an ESU (Emergency Services Unit) of 50 SWAT officers to assist in getting him to the building.

I was listening to the radio transmissions and the commotion on the streets was unprecedented. The streets around the UN were packed with people and for blocks cars could not drive on them, as a sea of humanity had taken over these roads.

As the NYPD and his security team walked him from his car to the UN building people began to recognize him and praise and loud applause could be heard for blocks. The cheers were so loud people thought that Elvis Presley came back from the dead.

As we waited for his arrival the UN general secretary brought out a large television for us to watch the scene on TV. As we were watching a breaking news alert flashed across the screen, it was the Pope at the Vatican. The scene quickly switched to the Pope speaking and asking for members of the Unity Religion to support the Assyrian President in his speech for a one-world economic system. At this point in time all Catholics, Muslims,

Buddhists, Hindus, and Mormons and even Scientologists were part of the Unity Religion and followed the Pope.

Within minutes of the Pope speaking the Assyrian President entered the building. Word came over the radio to open the exit door and let him enter through there. As I opened the door ESU officers started to come through, what a procession 50 NYPD and 20 of his own security, it took 11 minutes for all of them to enter the room.

There he was the Assyrian President - a 6'6" tall presence in the room like no other. When he walked in the room applause broke out and all the other heads of State began to cheer. He got a very friendly reception.

It took another 10 minutes before the cheers stopped and order could be restored to the room. Then he took the podium.

"Members of the UN general assembly welcome. For almost 3 years now I have been trying to unite the world with a one world government and religion. A united people that will bring world peace and prosperity to the world.

"In the nations that I control I have set up an electronic currency that has reduced crime, and stopped tax evasion. This has meant more prosperity for the people of my countries. This simple computer chip that is installed on a person's hand or head makes it easy for anyone to buy or sell. Furthermore, we can put all a person's medical records on it, so in case of a car accident the hospital will know your blood type and other lifesaving information. The advantages are so numerous!

"No more having to wait on checkout lines in supermarkets, simply scan and go. No more cash that can be stolen or robbed. So now it is time to make this system a worldwide system. The reason is simple - it works!!!

"Recently, people from America came to Europe to visit and were unable to use our subways and transit system because they did not have the ability to pay for things. Let us change the way the world works and come together in unity and join our one world economic system.

"My followers who have come here today to support me, please let out a big Unity scream and let President Harris know that she and the United States needs to join us in creating a one world economic system that benefits everyone!!!"

The applause from the streets could be heard in the room, the people outside were going wild - screaming for everyone to join the one world economy!!!

The Assyrian president then came off the podium to thunderous applause.

The UN general secretary came to the podium. He asked if there was anyone that wanted to speak in opposition to the Assyrian President's plan. Then President Chi of China asked to speak. He made his way to the podium to no applause.

President Chi looked at the audience and stated,

"The Chinese people for thousands of years have been a unique and special culture. Our warriors have defended our country, pride and since before Egypt existed. We will not compromise our culture for this one world government. The Chinese people will be governed by the Chinese. We have a 200,000,000-man army and our soldiers are ready and able to defend China from any threat foreign or domestic. We refuse to participate in this one-world order."

The audience was silent but the protesters on the streets of New York were going wild booing and causing havoc!!!

The UN General Secretary came to the podium and stated that no one would speak today and dismissed the assembly. Tomorrow President Yeltsin of Russia and President Harris of the USA speak.

Meanwhile the scene on the streets was getting out of control. Cars were being overturned and Asians were being attacked for no reason. One woman was attacked and beaten by 5 of the protesters. They beat her until she was lying on the ground unable to move. Brutal and beyond the pale of normality. I headed back to my room after my shift ended and went to sleep.

CHAPTER 18
THE U.N. DETAIL CONTINUES

WEDNESDAY, MARCH 5TH, 2031

Today at the UN President Yeltsin and President Harris were to speak. The protesters were chanting,

"One world government, one world religion and one world economic system!!!!"

The noise from the streets was so loud that the UN General Secretary had to delay the speeches. The police outside were struggling to control the crowds, last night 417 people were arrested for various reasons.

Finally, by 10:35am the UN General Secretary called on President Yeltsin to speak. President Yeltsin came to the podium and began to speak.

"Members of the UN, I stand before you and ask that we listen to the words of my friend President Chi and not follow the dictates of the Assyrian President. First, a one-world order will destroy a country's ability to govern itself. The Russian people are a proud people and for years invaders from Napoleon to Hitler have tried to conquer our nation, only to be turned back by the will of the Russian people. We love our nationality and culture.

"Secondly, the citizens of Russia feel that the Assyrian President wants to be worshipped and praised like Adolf Hitler before him. The Russian people will not do it.

"Thirdly, the economic system that the Assyrian President proposes will give him and his government the ability to shutdown or cancel anybody at any time. This means that freedom will be gone from the earth no one will be able to protest against the government or say anything against the Syrian president without losing their ability to buy or sell. All dissenters will be silenced and cut-off from all economic activity.

"Therefore, I am begging and pleading with each and every one of you to vote against this terrible plan of a one world economic system that forces every man, woman and child to get a chip implanted in their hand or forehead to be able to buy or sell. In Russia we have gone back to using silver and gold coins for currency and the people love it.

"Later today when we vote on this matter, I hope that you will not be influenced by the protesters outside in the streets, they are here to intimidate you and I hope it doesn't work."

To faint applause President Yeltsin left the stage.

A 2-hour lunch recess was announced. Afterwards President Harris will speak before tomorrow's vote. All Members will be given a night to think over the decision they must make. This vote is considered the most consequential in the history of the UN.

After we enjoyed a nice lunch in the UN cafeteria, I had the lamb chops with mint jelly.

Everyone came back to the meeting room to await the arrival of the US President, President Harris.

The crowd outside was chanting her name, the same people that came to support the Assyrian leader are here for her. They knew that she would support a one world economic system even at the cost of American Sovereignty. She has been close to the Assyrian President since her taking office in 2029.

However, under her leadership America has suffered - inflation, loss of credit rating due to massive spending and a $45 trillion debt. The country is run like Chicago in 1930. The entire country has gone downhill so fast - we are no longer the greatest country in the world. We have done nothing as the Assyrian President has expanded his territory and caused death, inflation and famine throughout the world.

With a rousing welcome President Harris came on stage and began to speak. She started with,

"Thank you leaders of the world,"

and the UN assembly rose to their feet and clapped wildly for her. She began by saying that she was from a poor middle class family but rose from the ashes to aspire to greatness. (She still talks in word salads). Then she got to the point,

"Since I took office, I have been a big admirer of the Assyrian President. He alone came back to life after being stabbed in the head by a rebel. He has worked with the Pope to bring about a Unity religion."

The roar of the crowds on the street could be heard in the room, then the assembly stood up to applaud. She stopped speaking to allow everyone to hear how they loved her. President Harris continued,

"Not since the beginning of time has a man brought people together, look outside and see all the support we have for a unified economic system. A system that guarantees lower taxes, lower costs and the simplicity of convenience in every transaction we make. Think about it, no one can steal your money!!! We all should take the MARK, it's simple and easy. Then anyone can travel anyplace in the world and never have to worry about exchanging money or being robbed.

"When I get back to Washington, I will ask congress to pass legislation that will make the MARK our national economic currency. With a democratic house and senate we will make it law!!"

Outside the demonstrators went wild, cheering and clapping. She concludes by saying,

"My fellow world leaders I implore you to vote for this universal one world system tomorrow!!"

She left the stage to thunderous applause. Then the secretary of the UN came to the stage to dismiss the assembly till tomorrow when the vote will occur.

CHAPTER 19
THE ONE WORLD SYSTEM

THE UN VOTES FOR A ONE WORLD ECONOMIC SYSTEM

Today is the last day of the Secret Service detail and the day for the UN to vote if they want a worldwide economic system or if they want to keep their own currency. They named the system the MARK because you must have a chip embedded in your forehead or hand. The chip works just like the chip in your credit card except it can't be stolen!

121 countries are present and each one has a vote. The UN General Secretary stated that he would call out the name of each country and they will vote Yay or Nay. To appease the massive crowds outside, they decided to put giant speakers outside so that the crowd could hear how each country voted. Every time a country voted No, boos could be heard from the crowd outside, but every time a country voted Yes, applause erupted outside. After a few hours, the votes were totaled and the final numbers were 74 for and 47 against.

The General Secretary got up to announce the final vote and said:

"The MARK economic system will be accepted in all nations."

He said that details of the transition will be given to the nations next month when details are finalized.

Following that announcement, the crowd outside went wild, cheering, screaming, and yelling—it sounded like the Yankees won the World Series.

At 3 p.m., the shift leader came to the Assembly and said the detail was over and told us to go home. He reminded us that money was tight, so in light of the situation, we were told to take tomorrow off because the Service was short on overtime money.

With that, I went to my room and packed my bags and checked out of the hotel. Then I traveled back home to Long Island.

I was home by 6 p.m. I went into the house and saw Diana on the couch crying. I was stunned that she was so upset. I asked:

"Why are you crying?"

She was crying uncontrollably, tears and sobs, and finally said:

"This is what the Bible said would happen. Unless we get the MARK, we won't be able to buy anything."

I asked her to please explain what is going to happen. She was too upset to talk, so I went to bed early, and we will discuss it tomorrow.

CHAPTER 20
MARK OF THE BEAST EXPLAINED

MARCH 7TH, 2031

Diana said:

"Bob, open the Bible to Revelation 13:16-17."

I read: "He required everyone—small and great, rich and poor, free and slave—to be given a mark on the right hand or on the forehead. And no one could buy or sell anything without that mark, which was either the name of the beast or the number representing his name."

Diana said:

"Now that the UN has voted to put this system in place, we are doomed!"

Diana explained:

"If we take the MARK, then we go to hell! Taking the MARK is like saying Heil Hitler—it is a form of worship to the Antichrist. It is why Jesus said, 'He who endures to the end shall be saved!'"

I felt sick. What were we going to do? I knew that with President Harris in office, everyone will be forced to take the MARK, and those that don't would be fired. I remembered in 2020 when hospital staff were fired for not taking the COVID shot. Hospital staff, of all people. Military fighter jet pilots were fired from the military—it was crazy—and now this!

I said:

"We have to pray."

So, for the next hour, we prayed and worshiped God. We knew that the Bible was right; we could not take the MARK, or we would be doomed. So, we made a list of what's the most important things we needed to survive:

1) We need a roof over our head. Must have housing.
2) Food—we need to eat to survive.
3) Transportation—must be able to travel.
4) Medical supplies—in case of sickness.
5) People we can trust—when people find out that we won't take the MARK, they will turn on us if they are not Christians.
6) A friend that has the MARK so that we can get items we need.
7) Gold and silver because for thousands of years they have been used as currency.

With a list and a plan, Diana and I agreed to begin preparing tomorrow by going to look at farmland out on the east end of Long Island.

CHAPTER 21
LIVING OFF GRID

SAT/SUN, MARCH 8/9, 2031

We got up early and headed out East towards Montauk. We are looking for at least 5 acres of farmland that we can grow crops and livestock. In addition, we plan to get 5 of those tiny homes to bring in revenue. We prayed for God's favor before we left the house and figured we would drive around the area before stopping into a realtor's office to see what was available. As we drove the local roads, we saw a farm stand that was unoccupied (it is March, and no fruits or vegetables are in season). In front of the stand was a For Sale by Owner sign. So, we called the number, and the man who answered was an 85-year-old man named Farmer Ed. Farmer Ed said he was the owner and wanted to sell. We asked if we could meet with him, and he said:

"Drive up the driveway and meet me at the barn."

So we did.

Farmer Ed was pleasant and invited us up to the house for coffee. We sat down, and Farmer Ed poured us coffee and started to explain why he was selling:

"Since the election in 2028, things have not gone well. Kids have been stealing my crops, and it's impossible to make ends meet. I have had to live off my savings the last 3 years, and working the farm isn't paying the bills. Years ago, I never had to worry about the crops being stolen, but now it's commonplace, and the police don't do anything. At my age, it's just best to sell and move on."

I asked Farmer Ed to show us the property and all the outbuildings like the barn. So, we went for the tour. 5 acres of farmland with a barn that used to house 2 horses but contained 3 stalls. A garage that was a big steel building that contained all the farming equipment, including a tractor, lawnmower, and pick-up truck, a 20-year-old F-150 Super Duty.

Farmer Ed said:

"Next year is the 7th year, which is a rest year for the land. 4 acres must be rested to build back the nutrients in the soil. 1 acre will be usable, and that acre will be rested the following year."

This is another reason he is looking to sell now. Farmer Ed said that he's owned the property since 1985 and bought it because he loved the natural spring that flows through the property.

We asked Farmer Ed if we can go to the car to discuss the matter. He said:

"Sure, take your time."

Diana and I went to the car, and I asked her what she thought. She said:

"I like it, but let's pray because only God knows if it's the right property for us."

I prayed:

"Father God, if it's the right property, let Farmer Ed sell it for less than $1,000,000."

Then, after we prayed, Diana said:

"I think we should witness to him and pray for him."

I agreed.

We went back to the house and asked Farmer Ed:

"Have you ever heard the gospel of Jesus Christ?"

He said:

"Yes, but when my wife died, I got mad at God and stopped believing."

I said:

"Would you like to pray for a miracle and get filled with the Holy Spirit?"

He said:

"Sure, at my age, I need a miracle."

Well, we prayed, and the Holy Spirit filled the room—it was amazing. Farmer Ed said:

"That has never happened before."

He was in awe. Then he made us an intriguing offer. We had discussed with him our plan to put 3 tiny homes on the property and the fact that I worked for the Secret Service. Farmer Ed said:

"Instead of paying me my $2,000,000 asking price, give me $200,000, but I get to live here the rest of my life, and you must put a fence around the property and stop the kids from stealing the crops. You can take the money that you don't have to pay me and use it to build the 3 tiny houses and the fence."

Diana and I excused ourselves and went out to pray. I asked her:

"Can we live in one of the tiny houses for a while?"

She said:

"Get the biggest tiny house you can, at least 3 bedrooms to give us the room we need. The others can be 1- or 2-bedroom ones."

We agreed to the following terms: We would buy the property for $500,000, and $300,000 of that would be used to pay for the fence and the tiny houses, and Farmer Ed lives the rest of his life in his home. This way, we have enough money to do it all.

Diana and I were excited because we knew that with my salary, getting a mortgage for that amount would be no problem. Now it was off to the bank to get the financing in place.

We left with a contract in hand and started our mortgage search at TD Bank. We left the house and went downtown to TD Bank. We walked in and asked to see the mortgage manager.

Based on my salary with overtime at the Secret Service, which is over $300,000, this made qualifying for the loan easy to do. The banker asked for last year's tax return and last week's pay stub. He also needed an appraisal. Upon submission of all documents, the closing can be set up within 4 weeks.

We left the bank happy and decided to spend the rest of the day shopping for supplies. First, we went to BJ's for bulk canned food. I wanted to make sure that we had enough canned food and water to last a year. Since Diana and I were able to figure out that the dispensation of grace or the tribulation period for the saints is 1260 days according to Revelation 12:6 and confirmed by Daniel 7:25 and Revelation 13:5.

Knowing that we were going to have to move, we decided to get half now and half after we buy the property and settle in there. After getting the food, a lot of tuna, bottled water, canned peaches, canned pineapple, applesauce, pasta, sauces, soups, supplies for camping, a lot of charcoal, and frozen food.

We took it all home and unpacked the car. Tomorrow, we get medical supplies, fishing poles, lanterns, blankets, and that sort of stuff.

Sunday morning: We started our day in prayer and worship. We asked God for guidance in what to get and where to get it. At 10 a.m., we were back in the car on the way to a super Walmart to get what we needed. We even found a solar generator that they were selling for a few thousand dollars. We bought fishing equipment, camping equipment like lanterns, blankets, sleeping bags, stoves for outdoor use. We just didn't know how bad it was going to get, so we prepared the best we could. We even bought a survival book and water purifier pills.

We bought solar chargers for the phones in case the electric was shut off. I already owned 12 guns and enough ammo to last 5 years, so that wasn't needed.

We came home exhausted but knowing that we were prepared, at least that's what we thought.

CHAPTER 22
THE NEW POLICY

SECRET SERVICE ANNOUNCES ITS POLICY ON THE MARK

Today is Friday, and I am in the office. Larry announced a group meeting at 11 a.m. to talk about a memo that came down out of Washington, D.C. The last few weeks have been so hectic trying to get ready for the move. I had anticipated that today would be the day I was dreading, and sure enough, it was.

At 11 a.m., we all assembled in the conference room, and Larry handed out the memo from Washington. The memo said that in order to be in compliance with the UN MARK mandate, every employee must receive the MARK by December 31st, 2031.

In order to speed up the process, the government was offering one week's pay for every month you get the MARK before December. So, anyone that gets it in April gets 9 weeks' pay added to their paycheck in the pay period after the employee receives the MARK. If you wait till May, you get 8 weeks' pay added. If you wait till December, you only get 1 week's pay added to your pay. If you don't have it by December 31st, then you get terminated, without the ability to collect unemployment or anything else. The memo said that the government is considering criminal charges against those that oppose and refuse to get the MARK. Larry also said that legislation is in Congress to stop printing money and demand that everything go digital. So, we can expect that all money not deposited into your bank will become worthless over the next few months.

Secret Service will continue to pay its employees through the direct deposit system through December 31st, 2031. After that, all pay will be deposited into your account associated with your MARK. If you don't have the MARK by then, you will not be paid, and if you refuse to get it, you must be terminated. No excuses and no exemptions.

Some of the guys in the office were excited about it and planned to get it next month to pick up 9 weeks' pay. But for me and a few others, we knew we were doomed. There was no way to accept the MARK and not go to hell. I realize I have to do everything I can to prepare because come December, I am unemployed.

CHAPTER 23
MOVING IN

WE CLOSE ON THE FARM AND MOVE IN**

Farmer Ed, Diana, and I met at TD Bank at 10 a.m. to get the loan proceeds and transfer the property. By 11:30, we were done. Farmer Ed is happy to have received enough money to pay his bills for life, and we are happy to have this property for 10% of its value. We immediately, after closing, went to the property to wait for the delivery of the tiny houses we ordered a few weeks ago. We planned their delivery with the closing. We put the down payment on the credit card, and now we have the money from closing to pay them off in full. At 2 p.m., the trucks started pulling in, and we had already prepared the places for them to be installed. We paid for full installation.

Farmer Ed has worked with us since March when we signed a contract to buy the property, so we were able to quickly get things done. The houses come prebuilt, and we had the water, sewer, and electric ready to be connected. When they came, it was a seamless operation to complete. By 8 p.m., we had flushing toilets and kitchen lights. Everything seemed to work perfectly. The advancements in technology made it a quick and easy process. Then we called the movers, who already had the truck packed, and told them to come on down. They were there by 9 p.m., and by 10 p.m., everything was unloaded off the truck, and we began to unpack boxes until exhaustion kicked in, and we passed out at 2 a.m.

Tuesday, April 22nd, 2031: We got up at about 11 a.m. to finish unpacking and getting everything set up. We like the new bed that we bought. The house itself is actually nicer than I thought it would be. The craftsmanship is excellent, and I am happy with the purchase.

Wednesday, April 23rd - Tuesday, May 6th, 2031: These two weeks were spent putting up the fence at the farm and getting the other 2 tiny homes furnished and in move-in condition. I took a few days off from work, and the days I did go in, I was catching up on paperwork. However, Wednesday, May 7th, will be different.

CHAPTER 24
END OF THE FIAT

U.S. TREASURY ANNOUNCES END TO U.S. CURRENCY AND CONGRESS PASSES LEGISLATION TO MAKE DIGITAL CURRENCY THE ONLY WAY TO BUY OR SELL**

Today is Wednesday, and I decided that I needed a day off, so I decided to complete the moving-in process by unpacking a few boxes that still needed to be put away.

As I was unpacking a box of kitchen dishes, I decided to put the television on. Suddenly, Breaking News! U.S. Treasury Secretary Ted Myers announces an end to Federal Reserve currency. A news conference was about to begin. The Treasury Secretary came to the podium and began a 15-minute speech. He stated:

"In order to bring about the MARK system on a timely basis, all U.S. Federal Reserve bills will be worthless by September 1st, 2031. If you have any cash, it must be deposited into the bank by then. As Treasury Secretary, I have ordered the IRS not to open any cases based on large cash deposits from now until September 1st."

He continued:

"We are not trying to develop tax cases; we are just looking for a smooth transition into the MARK system. In order to help with this transition, we are giving banks incentives to take in large deposits. Tomorrow, banks will be advertising the incentives. Some banks will match deposits dollar for dollar up to $10,000."

He added:

"Furthermore, Congress passed legislation that makes digital dollars the only valid currency. So, by September 1st, we will be on our way to making the MARK the only economic system. The legislation provides funding for all businesses to order and receive MARK readers by November 30th, 2031. This will give businesses time to learn to operate and use the new readers. This will guarantee that by December 31st, 2031, no one will be able to buy or sell unless they have the MARK. Without the MARK, you will not be able to enter a store because you won't be able to buy anything. This system will stop theft and guarantee lower prices for all people. If someone is caught stealing with the MARK, the cost of the stolen goods will be automatically taken from their account."

He concluded:

"Filing a tax return will be a thing of the past; income tax will be replaced with a sales tax and will be easy to enforce. This will give us the unity that America was founded on. President Harris looks forward to the day when all citizens are one and have one MARK!"

What a news conference. I was sick to my stomach! Now I know that if I get the MARK, my eternal destiny is hell, or I will starve to death if I don't! Jesus said:

"Those who endure until the end shall be saved."

I am so thankful that the Bible tells us exactly how long the tribulation will last. Gotta last to March 12th of next year. I think that is doable. Then the catching up of all those that are alive and have been faithful to God will be taken to heaven. Diana and I read this verse every day—Revelation 7:9:

"After this, I saw a vast crowd, too great to count, from every nation and tribe and people and language, standing in front of the throne and before the Lamb." These are all of the believers alive today waiting for the 1260 days to end. We know this because in Revelation 7:14, which in summary says these are the ones who came out of the great tribulation.

With all the raptured saints preaching the gospel and the hatred for the Christians and Jews and anyone who refuses to worship the Assyrian President is seen as a horrible, terrible person, we can't wait for this time to come to an end.

Now to prepare to live without the MARK!

CHAPTER 25
MANDATORY POST MARK

CITIZENS ORDERED TO REPORT TO POST OFFICES TO RECEIVE THE MARK

Today, I was in the office doing paperwork when my supervisor, Larry, asked to see me in his office. I sat down, and he said:

"I have a special detail for you to do."

He said that me and a few other agents will be doing security at the local post office for the next few weeks.

President Harris has issued a memo that mandates that all citizens report to their local post office to receive the MARK. Teams of specialists will be there to administer the MARK to local citizens. Those that show up within the first 90 days will be given a $1,000 bonus added to their account.

I went to the post office as assigned and had to work outside security. People were showing up in mass.

To my surprise, people are willing and able to sign up; they can't wait to get the extra money.

I also noticed a small group of 7 protesters that was meeting on the north lawn of the post office. I went up to them and introduced myself:

"I'm Special Agent Bob Klement with the United States Secret Service."

I explained to them that any type of protest must be peaceful and contained to public property. The leader of the group, a guy named Sam, said:

"Do you know that this is the Mark of the Beast! Anybody that takes this Mark will go to hell. This is what Revelation 13 was talking about 2000 years ago."

Sam said:

"We must tell people not to take this Mark."

I said:

"Sam, I am between a rock and a hard place—I agree with you, but I am in my capacity as a Special Agent with the U.S. Secret Service, and I have to make sure that no protests get out of hand."

I said:

"Look, if arguing starts, someone will call the local PD, and they will come looking to bust heads. I will do all I can to support your right to voice your opinion, but it can't get out of hand."

The lines kept growing, so many people there to collect the $1,000 bonus. Sam and his group had signs that read: "The MARK of the Beast is here," "If you take it, you go to hell," "Repent and believe in the Lord Jesus Christ —Lord of Lords and King of Kings." As the protesters stood outside with their signs, it was only a matter of time before they drew a crowd.

Another agent came outside to see what was going on—he said:

"They could hear the commotion from inside the building."

He asked if I needed backup, and I said:

"No, I got it under control."

He said:

"We can get another 6 agents on site if we need it."

I told him that I would handle these protesters. He could go back inside, and if I needed him, I would radio for assistance.

I am always diligent about having my vest and secondary weapons like pepper spray and my baton in case of trouble. I also hung an extra badge around my neck if I needed to immediately identify myself. With that said, I watched as three men wearing biker attire with patches on their jackets that read "Hell's Children."

One of these men went up to Sam and called him a Christian faggot and spit on him. Another woman in the crowd called 911. I was close enough to hear her conversation. She said:

"There is a group of protesters here at the Post Office with signs that I find offensive. My feelings are being violated, and I want the police to come and arrest them. Their offensive signs say Jesus is King, and we all know that's a lie. The Pope said we need to worship the Assyrian President, so please send the police."

I knew that I would have to act before things got too out of control. So, I first approached the guy with the Hell's Children patch. I exposed my badge that I had around my neck and asked to speak with him. He said:

"Who the hell are you?"

I stated:

"I am Bob Klement with the U.S. Secret Service, and we are here to keep the peace."

I told him that we had 12 agents on site and that spitting on protesters or any kind of physical altercation would result in removal or arrest.

He says:

"Fuck you, what are you going to do?"

So, I laugh at him and say:

"Nothing, absolutely nothing. I am going to call Bubba Johnson, our biggest and baddest agent. He's inside with 6 other agents—he's 6'9" and a 2x Mr. America, absolutely loves violence. He looks for a reason to arrest scum like you. So, if you want to wait a few minutes, I will call, and the crew will come out."

At that moment, I pretended to get on the radio, but I didn't push the transmit button and said:

"Bubba, we have a situation. I have a Hell's Children with his 2 friends that are assaulting and spitting on protesters. They need to be arrested and taught a lesson. Please come out with the crew and take care of the situation. Please promise me that you won't beat him to death like you did the last 4 bikers. What do you mean you can't promise? Yes, I know how much you hate those scum bags. Ok, I won't let him get away."

At that point, I looked this guy in the eyes and said:

"Why don't you just get out of here before those agents come out that door. They will make an example out of you; they will show you no mercy. You may be in hell within the next 2 hours. Think about it. Don't mess with the Feds."

He looks at me and says:

"Fuck you."

Then tells his friends:

"Let's go."

And gets on his motorcycle and takes off—quicker than a speeding bullet.

I thought that after they left, I would catch a break, but no—the police sirens were loud, and 3 police cars showed up. They immediately went over to the protesters and started questioning them about their signs. I approached the lead police officer and identified myself:

"I'm the lead Special Agent in charge of the site."

The police officer said that they were responding to a call and wanted to arrest the protesters. I explained to the police that the post office was a federal building, and we had jurisdiction here. They said that they had a complaint, and the signs were probable cause. I asked to speak to the complainant. They brought her over to me.

I said:

"You called the police and want the protesters arrested, is that correct?"

She said that their signs were causing her emotional stress, and she feels violated. I said:

"The Secret Service is in charge of protecting this building, and if you want to follow through on that complaint, I will be forced to arrest you for criminal trespass on federal property."

I then called for assistance, and 3 agents came out to assist. I took them aside and told them what's going on. I explained how this woman was causing issues, so I asked them to surround her. I then asked the woman:

"What do you want to do?"

She looked at the three agents and said:

"I feel violated."

I said:

"You don't know what that word really means—what do you want to do?"

Then I called the cop over and told him what was going to happen, and he asked her what she wanted to do. She said:

"Forget it, I just want to go home and cry."

I then asked the police to leave, and they did. The woman, still crying, ran for her car, but it was noticeable that she had peed her pants in the process of leaving.

I realized how out of control the situation was getting, so I approached Sam and told him:

"I agree that your cause is noble, and people need to know the consequences of taking the MARK, but the police are looking for a reason to arrest you, so it would be best if you left and came back another day."

Sam could see the attitude of the police when they arrived. He knew that they were looking for a reason to arrest them and do them harm. It didn't make sense for them to hang around and wait for someone else to call, so they agreed to leave.

After they did, my tour of duty was over. I went home to Diana and watched the news and saw the number of people showing up to get the MARK.

We enjoyed a nice steak dinner and spoke about our role in telling people about the consequences of getting the MARK. I said:

"Diana, do you remember COVID and how many people took the shot? Remember we had friends that died from complications, but could we save them?"

"No," she said, "because fear of them losing their jobs or fear of the virus."

I continued:

"We told everyone we could about the possible consequences, but people did it anyway. I feel the same way about this; we can and will warn them, but they will make the final decision."

We agreed that's about the best we can do and decided to go to bed.

CHAPTER 26
THE NEW COLONY

SETTING UP THE FARM AND PREPARING FOR THE NEW ECONOMY

After seeing how the people were responding at the post office, I realized that living without the MARK is going to be very, very tough. I am truly amazed at how gullible people are; without any thought for eternity, they are just willingly signing up and taking the MARK to have $1,000 added to their bank account. I need God's wisdom on how to plan for the next year. I am so thankful that the Bible tells us that the tribulation is only 1260 days. I am amazed I made it this far without too much turbulence.

Diana and I have been living at the farm for over a month now. We are living in a 3-bedroom home that is almost 2,000 square feet. Not a bad size. The other homes are 2 bed, 2 bath for rental or family and friends.

We made sure that both water and electric won't be an issue. We have city water with a backup well in case we can't pay the water bill. Electricity, we put solar panels and small windmills on the corner of each house. We had to enclose the windmill like a fan so no birds fly into it accidentally. We also have a battery in each home to store the power so if it snows and the panels get covered or if no sunlight is available, we will still have electricity. I even went one step further and ordered a Generac home generator for the main house where Farmer Ed lives and our 3-bedroom home. That has a gas fuel tank that will supply power for 3 full months if power is lost. So, for now, I am still connected to the city power, but my bill is only $12 a month. So, we are almost totally self-sufficient. I am trying to prepay for electric and water for the next year so when I don't take the MARK, I will continue to receive services.

I hired a carpenter to come to the house to create a hidden room in the house. He saw my car and noticed the police lights and asked:

"Are you a cop?"

I told him:

"I work with the Secret Service, and in case I have to protect a dignitary, I need a hidden room."

So, he said:

"That makes sense."

And we decided to use half of the 3rd bedroom. He built a false wall that would slide open and could be locked from the other side. In that room, I will keep all my firearms, bulletproof vests, bottled water, medical supplies, a small heater and air cooler. I also have walkie-talkies and a radio, a porta-potty, and mattresses in case Diana and I have to stay there a while. I also will put a week's worth of food, just in case. I put 5 days' worth of clothes for Diana and me in the half of the closet that was in the hidden room. Trying to prepare for any eventuality.

Next step was setting up a greenhouse. I recognize the ability to grow food is absolutely essential. So, next to the greenhouse, we will put a steel building that will act as a garage and a place to freeze-dry the food that we grow; this will guarantee food in the winter. I ordered equipment to can and freeze food that we grow. In addition to growing fruits and vegetables, we will need meat. A chicken coop and a pig pen will also be welcome additions. Chickens will lay eggs and can be easily turned into a meal. Pigs and hogs can be easily butchered.

I was very fortunate to have become friends with the butcher in town; for a small fee, he will slaughter and butcher chickens and hogs for me.

I thought about cows but didn't think it would be feasible; too big to butcher, and they crap a lot.

Today, a news flash came across the television at 2 p.m. A new virus just broke out in Europe. This new COVID strand is worse than the one from 2020. The news was calling for people to go to their local pharmacy and get vaccinated. But Diana and I know the problems the vaccine caused for many who took it. It was designed to change your DNA and not stop the virus. So, instead, we bought medical kits with Ivermectin and other products to help us survive. We have been counting the days until the dispensation of grace ends, and we have 9 months left to survive. Many Christians have already been killed, but with my job with the Secret Service and the grace of God, we have survived so far.

CHAPTER 27
SUMMER REVIVAL

GOD POURS OUT HIS SPIRIT ON ALL FLESH

This diary entry is for all of the month of July. It has been quite crazy to see how God has sent a revival in the land amongst the craziness of the government. It started on Tuesday night, July 1st, 2031. A small group of Christians in Idaho set up speakers in a cornfield. They started to blast praise music and left the field. Then people started to show up from all around to see what was going on. Before you know it, a crowd gathered. Suddenly, and without warning, as the crowd gazed into the sky, a group of raptured saints appeared and started to preach the gospel of Jesus Christ. People were moved and started to respond, then the police showed up in force, but the saints just preached the word, and the police fell down, experiencing the spirit of God and couldn't move. When the people saw the power of God, they came forward in mass. This was the beginning of a movement. Some of the people that accepted Christ decided to do the same thing in other states, and by mid-July, hundreds of praise sites broke out throughout the country. The police were unable to stop it because every time a crowd broke out, a raptured saint showed up to preach, and their words nullified anything the police could do.

The theme was always the same:

"Repent of your sins and believe on the Lord Jesus Christ, and you shall be saved! God loves people and wants them to inherit eternal life."

When Diana and I sat down to study the Bible, we were asking each other the same question:

"How is it in Revelation 7:9-14 that so many millions come to know Jesus and make it through the terrible times we are living through now?"

Then the answer came to us:

"It's those raptured saints that so many of us knew and the word of their testimony that gives us the strength to live and overcome until the Lord comes for us."

Riots and chaos were starting to break out in the major cities as the power of God was seen. The Unity church members came out in force to cause violence and chaos. Every night on the news, another city and new riots. Yet hope came upon us as we saw the move of God take place. By the end of July, many people had come to know Jesus and were refusing to take the MARK.

This made the next few months chaotic throughout the country, then September 11th happened.

CHAPTER 28
THREE YEARS AFTER THE RAPTURE

THREE YEARS SINCE THE RAPTURE

Thursday, September 11th, 2031

It has been a few months since I have last made a diary entry. With all that has been happening with the Assyrian President, they have kept me quite busy. I have been working a lot of protection details; twelve hours a day, six and sometimes seven days a week, protecting dignitaries from all over the world. Since I work in the New York field office we are responsible for protecting any dignitary that comes to the USA and most go to the UN so that falls upon the NY Field Office to provide protection.

As a result of all the wars commodity prices have gone crazy. Disease has taken the lives of 15% of the world's population, mostly in the countries at war with the Assyrian President. Life here in the USA has gotten really bad too. The socialist policies have created high unemployment and very high tax rates, up to 90%.

Today has been three years since the Saints have been caught up to God. The president of Assyria has taken control of Europe, Saudi Arabia, most of Africa, and Indonesia. But he is not the only one waging war. Today an invasion on Israel occurred. Russia, Kazakhstan, Iran, Turkey, Libya and Jordan all declared war on Israel. An Israeli jet shot down a Russian jet and an Iranian jet that violated its airspace during a training exercise. This event escalated and now these countries have decided to invade Israel. They put the Secret Service on high alert and I ended up doing some overtime.

Today, in New York they are having the 9/11 parade but it's not the same parade as 20 years ago when we remembered the twin towers being destroyed, instead people celebrate the Christians being removed from the earth, over a million people came to the city to celebrate. They are far left Unity Religion groups that hate Jews and Christians. They are here to make a statement and that statement is that they will overcome and be victorious over the people coming to Christ. They hate everyone and anyone that has accepted Jesus or professes him. With the revivals springing up all over the nation since July they have mobilized and come to the 9-11 parade to show the strength of the unity religion. With them comes violence and anarchy. They are using small frozen bottles of water - 8oz size and throwing them at the police and anyone they believe is a Christian or Jew. They carry knives and sometimes guns but since the police installed the new shot location finder, which identifies where the shot comes from and immediately takes a picture of the shooter, you don't get as much gun fire.

The Secret Service was tasked with identifying some of the worst agitators and getting intel for NYPD. I found myself out on Madison and 5th Avenue keeping an eye on a few of them. I was amazed at the hate they have for people and the evil deeds they do. As I stood on the corner, I watched a few of these people throwing water bottles at the police and then running into the subway to escape.

It was a long and sad day watching the city of New York being given over to these people.

Friday, September 12th, 2031

I went into the office to do my time sheet for the week. I was sitting at my desk when Larry announced a group meeting at 10am. So I got a cup of coffee and a muffin and reviewed my emails before the meeting began.

When we got into the conference room Larry announced the presence of the Deputy District Director of the Secret Service, Angelo Paparelli. Angelo was a leftover from the Trump administration and known for his competence and brilliance. He stopped an assassination attempt against President Harris in the summer of 2028, so she made sure she kept him on the job. Angelo was always well liked by the Agents but today he came bearing bad news. After the brief introduction He stated,

"Since the MARK system has been approved by President Harris and the UN, we must seek compliance. I have known a lot of you for many years and I never thought that we would see a day like today. However, President Harris has signed an executive order mandating ALL FEDERAL EMPLOYEES receive the MARK by December 31st 2031 or be terminated. No Exceptions. Therefore, in order for the Service to move forward with enough manpower to do our job, we need to know Today who has the MARK, who is getting the MARK and who will be terminated on December 31st. So, before you leave the office today, please state in writing what your intentions are. For those of you who decide to be terminated you will be given a check for your annual leave but not sick leave. However, you will not be entitled to any Unemployment compensation because you are making the decision to fire yourself and not be compliant."

After the meeting I went into Larry's office and gave him my written statement of termination. I said,

"Larry, this is the MARK of the beast that the bible talks about and I can't take it."

Larry said,

"Bob, I like you so I will write you a good guy letter so that you can get your gun permit here in New York City, at least that way you can protect yourself. Other than that, there is little that I can do."

I went home depressed knowing that come December life was going to be unbearable. I won't be able to go into any store in the city without the MARK. I will have no way to buy or sell. I need to get everything I can before December rolls around.

CHAPTER 29
STARVING WITHOUT THE MARK

NO ONE CAN BUY OR SELL WITHOUT THE MARK**

Today was my last day at work. I went in early to get everything handed in. Larry was very nice and he understood my position. I was one of 7 Agents in the office that refused to take the MARK. Larry wrote us all a good guy letter so that we could get our pistol permits. We also got checks for our unused vacation time. Starting tomorrow Every store in the country will not let you in unless you have the MARK.

So, after handing in my badge and my gun I went to see Ed Myers who is a special Agent in charge of selling secret service courtesy badges and lapel pins. I bought a bunch of them. It was truly depressing, knowing that I am now unemployed and unable to buy or sell anything after today. So, I got out of the office by 2 pm and went home to pick up Diana and we went shopping.

We know from the Bible that the time we have left on earth is only a few months away, as a matter of fact the exact date is March 12th 2032. That is 1260 days from the time that the saints disappeared and according to Revelation 7:9-14 all the saints get caught up to heaven. So, the plan is - buy everything necessary to make it to then.

We purchased a 90 supply of water and food, 2 electric generators, medical supplies and enough gas to power our hybrid vehicles for 4 months. We already had laundry soap and paper supplies so I think that I have all the bases covered.

We also have walkie talkies and an electric radio for emergencies.

After a long and depressing day, losing my job and my ability to buy and sell anything, I was in no mood to celebrate New Year's Eve. So, Diana and I decided to relax and watch the festivities on Television.

We didn't know that people would use this opportunity to celebrate our misfortune. There were celebrations in Times Square and the people were talking about how great it is that anyone that refused the MARK can't buy or sell.

One guy decided to get a posse together and go and kill Christians and Jews. I made sure the shotgun was at the door and I was ready. I don't believe in being a victim so I am always prepared.

However, channel 16 wanted to follow him and his posse and see if they can find any Christians. Diana wanted to turn the channel but I said,

"We have to watch and pray. If they are doing this now, what will they be doing tomorrow."

Their posse grew to about a dozen people and after 30 minutes they came across a young couple in their twenties, they had a sign repent and believe on the one true God Jesus Christ. The posse surrounded them and started cursing and spitting on them. Then the leader of the group said,

"Let's see if your Jesus can save you from the sewer."

He told 4 of the others to lift up the sewer grate and,

"Let's throw them in."

It took 6 of them to remove the grate, then the couple tried to flee but the woman was captured and the guy had to try to fight off 4 other guys. The camera was going back and forth between the action. They took the woman and threw her into the sewer and she was screaming,

"Help me! Help me!"

Then they replaced the sewer grate and left her there, in the sewer screaming, not strong enough to lift the grate and free herself. Then the camera went back to the man, he was beaten unconscious. Laying in the street on his back. They kicked him and spit on him and left him for dead in the middle of the road. Then 3 of the guys went to piss in the sewer. Truly evil despicable people.

Diana said,

"I can't watch anymore."

We decided to pray and ask God for grace and mercy because as of tomorrow we will be targets for people like this.

I really feel like it's just us against the world.

CHAPTER 30
LIVING WITHOUT A JOB

JANUARY 1ST, 2032

I didn't want to get out of bed today. I am unemployed and unable to shop.

I decided to get up and turn on the television. The news was showing the hand readers being installed in all the stores and supermarkets. In order for the door of the store to open it has to read the MARK on your hand or forehead. The TV commentator was speaking with the store manager on how it works and why they are installing the readers. According to the store manager that was interviewed he said that in order to be in compliance with the law of the MARK signed into law last year by President Harris all retail establishments must have readers installed. Without the MARK people can't even get into the stores. At gas stations new pumps were installed so that you have to put your hand on the pump to release it to buy gas. No more running into the store and telling the clerk to put $20 on pump 3. As a matter of fact, gas stations can now run with just one employee, whose job is to restock the shelves and keep the floors clean. The MARK system makes it almost impossible to steal anything. If you leave the store without paying it automatically charges your account when you get 10 feet outside the store.

At the malls there were protests from people that refused to get the MARK but counter protesters came out in greater numbers and started throwing frozen water bottles at them. Then they decided to use tear gas to disperse the protesters who were against the MARK.

While the TV commentator was describing the scene, suddenly two raptured saints appeared about 8 feet above the ground, they started preaching belief on the Lord Jesus Christ,

"DON'T get the MARK."

They said that the time for the dispensation of grace to end is close at hand. They brought encouraging words to the protestors that did not receive the MARK. Then they decreed disaster for those that did. The saints said,

"You fool, you have sold your souls for food and drink. Don't you know that the asteroid Apophis will hit the Americas in only a few short months and all who received the MARK will certainly perish."

The camera man was fixated on the two saints and so was everyone else. As a result, the crowd dispersed and the scene changed back to the television studio.

At this point I knew that I had work to do. I went out to the garage and took inventory of the gasoline that I had on hand. 125 gallons should be enough to last a few months for Diana and I but who knows how many people we will have to help. I topped off my old Avalon with 5 gallons of gas. Tomorrow, I have to go to Suffolk County Police, pistol licensing and see about getting my full carry permit.

Friday, January 2nd, 2032

When I arrived at the Pistol licensing section, I was told that there was a $100 fee for retired law enforcement officers and you must have the MARK to pay. I asked the clerk, a beautiful woman named Ivette. Ivette is always nice and cheerful with a great disposition, if lieutenant Craig Webkie was available. Craig and I were friends since Jr. High School, we were both on the cross-country team, a team that never lost a race in the 3 years I was there. Ivette went to get Craig, who was in charge of the unit. Craig was glad to see me, he said,

"Let's go out for coffee."

So, Craig and I drove to a diner and he agreed to pay since I don't have the MARK. We talked about how crazy things have become and he said he was forced to get the MARK or lose his job. I told him I lost my job because I won't get the MARK. I explained to him what the bible says about the tribulation period and how it is set to end on March 12th. He said,

"Maybe God would show him favor if he helped others."

I told him about the seven other Secret Service Agents that were fired for the same reason. He said,

"Call them and have everyone in my office tomorrow at 11am. Bring 4 silver dollar coins each and he would process and pay for everyone's fees."

Craig paid the diner bill and dropped me off at my car. I immediately called the other former Agents and told them what they needed to do.

Saturday, January 3rd, 2032

I told the other former Secret Service Agents what Craig proposed, they all agreed to meet at the Pistol Licensing bureau at 11am. When we arrived, Craig was there to meet us. We all gave Craig 4 one-ounce silver coins in exchange for him paying our processing fees. By 3pm we all had our full carry pistol licenses. With the license we were able to get our HR 218 training (the law that allows retired / law enforcement officers to carry in all 50 States).

Craig was able to take us through the 50 round qualification course and so we all ended up with both our pistol license and our HR218 qualification cards. We all gave Craig 2 more Silver coins for doing us the favor.

After that we all wanted to go out to dinner. However, we realized that we couldn't go out to dinner because we had no way to pay for it. So, I decided to invite everyone to my place for a barbeque. Craig joined us. I made sure that we had plenty of food for the next few months. I defrosted hot dogs, hamburgers and buns. The garage had plenty of water and drinks for everyone.

As I fired up the grill and started cooking, we started talking about how strange things have become. We took the time to pray and ask God for strength to endure this tough time. We all realize that we will never be able to walk into another store again. Never be able to buy or sell, instead we must survive by barter and mercy; thank God I stocked up but who knows what will be needed in an emergency. It was nice to know that I have friends like Craig to help out in times like these. After the burgers everyone left and Diana and I got to thinking just how difficult the next few months will be.

Monday, January 5th, 2032

Today the phone rang early 8am - it was Angelo Paparelli from the Secret Service. He called to inform me that he just got word from the white house that President Harris was going to sign an Executive order mandating the location of all non-MARKED people. Angelo said,

"This was bad, after locating all these people what would they do???? Arrest them, shoot them, he didn't know."

Angelo said he would call President Harris to get more clarity and get back to me. He said that if arrests are planned then he will get waivers from the president so that all his former Agents will be protected.

Without the ability to buy or sell there is nothing to do but read the bible, pray and wait for the end.

Tuesday, January 6th, 2032

At 10am I got a call from Frank Nardiello, a former secret service agent who left the service when I did because he refused to get the MARK. Frank stated that his electricity went off and he has no way to pay the bill. Frank is single and renting a house but it looks like he won't be able to stay there. I told him that I still have two tiny houses on the back of the property with solar for electric and well water for water. I told him that we could better protect the property and ourselves if he was here with us. I told him that Angelo called and an arrest order might be coming down the pike for us soon. Furthermore, I have seen roving gangs in the streets trying to harm Christians, with our weapons and training we can fend them off better together. Frank stated that he does have an arsenal and if we needed another agent or two, he knows who to call. I told Frank that I have to pray about it with Diana and I would get back to him tomorrow.

Diana and I talked about it and we decided that having two other former Special Agents from the Secret Service is a good idea. In addition to Frank,

I am going to call Dominic Trimboli. Dominic is a monster of a man 6'6" 290 solid muscles. Tough as nails, looks like Luca Brasi from the Godfather movie. One time he was protecting a dignitary from Pakistan when 2 Dobermans got loose and went after the protectee - Dominic got in front of him grabbed the dog's heads and smashed them together - just like in the movie True Lies with Arnold. The dogs lay there for a minute and then scampered off. Another time in Manhattan a protester went after the protectee and Dom grabbed him by the throat, planted him against a building and squeezed so hard his body went limp. Dominic is the guy you want on your side. One time we were working together protecting the Queen of Sweden, doing outside security while she was eating at a fancy 5-star Manhattan restaurant. Three guys approach us; they were MMA fighters. They just fought and won a bout at Madison Square Garden. They noticed our lapel pins, which of course have the secret service seal on them. They started to call us out,

"We will kick your ass, you're not so tough, all that kind of stuff."

The main guy said he was the undefeated heavyweight MMA champion 16-0 and he wanted to fight both of us. Dominic said,

"Bob, you fight him first."

I looked at him like you're kidding right. I said,

"OK, you want to fight, go for it."

When the MMA champion squared up to fight me, Dominic cold cocked him in the temple. He went out cold, never saw it coming. Then his friend tried to hit Dominic and he knocked him out. Third guy he made a step forward and Dominic kicked him so hard in the groin he couldn't get up.

This was Manhattan and it didn't take the police long to show up. We had them booked on assault charges and told the police to send us the report and if the US Attorney wants to press additional charges, we will issue a warrant and arrest them at that time. The Secret Service always had a good reputation with NYPD and occasionally you will get some tough guy that wants to challenge you. So we have to have each other's back. There was one incident when 2 female cops got attacked by a gang of 5 guys and Dominic was there to save them. He knocked out all 5 of them within 2 minutes. Those 2 cops made sure everyone knew who he was and NYPD gave him an award for his heroics. So, the cops were always on our side. Now you have an idea why I want Dominic Trimboli to move into the other guest house. I have enough food and supplies and it only makes sense to have enough people to protect the place.

Wednesday, January 7th, 2032

A cold freezing day here in New York. I got up praised God and prayed, I felt a release about having Frank and Dominic move into the 2 guest houses. Three former Secret Service agents are better than 1 protecting the property. The solar panels were working well even in this cold weather so we were able to keep warm. I called Frank to give him my decision. Frank was another giant of a man. Played college football, Center at Notre Dame. Not as big as Dominic but a very funny witty guy. He is always a joy to have around. Also, a really good shot, for two years he was a sniper for the President's protection team, back when Trump was President. He can shoot the pen out of your pocket from a mile away; another asset to have on the property. I really feel that God is bringing us together so that we can protect ourselves and others. As I reflected on scripture Luke 22:36 came to mind. When Jesus told the disciples to sell their cloak and buy a sword. The purpose of a sword is to defend oneself and that is what I believe we must do. The evil of the world and this government, where good is evil and evil is good. The righteous are hunted and killed and the guilty escape justice. I can't even imagine what would happen to Diana if these evil mobs had their way. No, we will stand and defend.

Thursday, January 8th, 2032

I called Dominic and I proposed that he come here and take the second guest house. He was getting sick of being alone and thought that it was a good idea. I told him to move in on Saturday. He agreed. Then I called Frank and told him to come on Saturday too, but Frank is without electricity so he asked to come tomorrow, so I said,

"Sure, see you when you get here."

Friday, January 9th, 2032

Frank showed up early to move in. I put him in guest house #1. He brought a lot of equipment and asked about setting up a sniper nest on the property. Like I said before he was a sniper on Trump's protection team. We scouted the property and found a big oak that had potential. With a little modification we can make it work. That will be for a warmer day. Frank also had a bunch of motion activated lights that we could set up around the property. He had a box of 50 which is more than enough to give us a heads up when people are on the property. In addition, he had several drones that he used for surveillance so we had 3 of those.

Frank and I spent the day moving in his stuff while Diana cooked. It was nice to have company and tomorrow the final piece will be added when Dominic shows up. We ate a nice steak dinner and went to bed early because tomorrow will be another busy day.

Saturday, January 10th, 2032

Today Dominic showed up to move in. He got guest house number 2. He also had a bunch of nice equipment, such as walkie talkies, automatic weapons and chemical weapons like tear gas. Dominic also had food and water and other supplies including a backup solar generator.

Between the 3 of us we have enough to withstand a mob. We feel like lepers, we can't go shopping, people hate us because we are not part of the global worship of the Anti-Christ. Everything is scarce, inflation is high, disease has come over from Europe and the love of many has grown cold. People don't care about people anymore. We realize that in the very near future we will be targeted. The only thing we can do is prepare.

We spent the day getting both Frank and Dominic moved in and situated in their new tiny homes.

Sunday, January 11th, 2032

Today we put on worship music and praised God for 2 hours. We put some of the automatic lights around the property and reviewed how to use the drones and we each placed one drone in each house. This way we could get one in the sky from each location if need be. We had dinner at my house and we reviewed the calendar to make sure that our dates are correct. Everyone agreed March 12th is the day. That is the end of the 1260 days from the date of the rapture. At the end of that day Revelation 7:9 takes place and millions upon millions of people are seen in heaven, rejoicing giving God glory because they just came out of great tribulation. Once that happens God's judgment is about to hit the earth - say hello to my little friend - Apophis!! According to Revelation 8 and Revelation chapter 16 it destroys 1/3 of all the trees, that's the Americas. So, we all know that those that have taken the MARK have a very short time before they are destroyed.

Diana, myself, Dominic and Frank found this very humbling and we praised and worshiped God praying for strength to endure the next 2 months. If we didn't know the bible we would have no end in sight. Knowing when this terrible time will end gives us hope and encouragement.

Monday, January 12th, 2032

Angelo Paparelli called to tell me that he spoke with President Harris and she is going to sign an executive order on February 1st 2032 mandating that all non-Marked people disclose their locations to local law enforcement. If they don't comply within 30 days they will be charged with Interference of Government administration. Angelo was also able to secure 150 waivers for this order to be given to former Secret Service Agents and their friends and family. We lost a total of 82 Agents at the end of last year when you had to have the MARK to continue to work there. Angelo said that they might be testing the AI electronic dog system before the order actually gets signed so that they will be ready to roll as soon as it becomes law. Angelo gave me his 24/7 cell number and told me to give it to Frank and Dominic, that way he can handle any static that may come our way.

I met with Frank and Dominic and we discussed what we had to do to prepare for the days ahead. We decided that we needed to get the sniper nest built. We are going to use the old oak tree and make it usable. We also needed to set up the food processing equipment in the garage area. If we had to butcher a hog, we needed to be able to freeze dry the meat and vacuum seal it to be frozen.

Tuesday, January 13th, 2032

Frank, Dominic and I got to work, it was a relatively warm day for January in New York, about 45 degrees, we spent hours setting up the sniper nest in the old oak tree. We set it up so 2 of us would be able to get up in the tree and snipe from North, East, South and West.

Dominic told us that he found 4 Burna guns as he was unpacking. The Burna guns shoot pepper balls that act as tear gas and are a great non-lethal weapon. He also found 155 rounds of the ammo for those guns. Dom also had a few cases of bird shot for the shotguns as well as a case of law enforcement loads. Additionally, Dominic found 6 Gas Masks which would be great if we needed to use the Burna guns. After assessing our equipment, we thought it would be a good idea to make a makeshift fence by using rope and posts. We had a lot of rope and about 20 posts that were on the property before we bought it. Farmer Ed showed us where it all was and helped us set it up on the property. This way we can be certain if someone is on our property or not. We used a motion light by each post, so the light will go on when someone steps on the property. It was a long day but we accomplished a lot. Next few days will be much of the same.

Friday, January 16th, 2032

The last few days were just preparing to defend the property in the event of a mass attack but today something happened that was totally unexpected. We had just finished dinner and the sun had gone down as the night air fell over the property, I went outside and saw the strangest sight. A robot dog standing on the driveway. It had red glowing eyes and just stood there. I called Frank and Dominic and asked them to come over. When they arrived, Dominic approached the robot but it didn't move; instead, another Robot dog came running up the driveway. The robots didn't make any noises - absolute silence. It was strange - why are they here and what are they doing. We debated calling the police but decided against it. Then after 15 minutes the robot dog requested that we show it our MARK. Of course, that was impossible because none of us has the MARK. The robot responded,

"You have 2 minutes for compliance."

And began a countdown until the 2 minutes were up. That's when the bells and whistles started to go off,

"Subject not in compliance, subject not in compliance, alert alert!!!"

Then red, white and blue lights started to flash from the robot and after about 30 seconds of the lights going off another verbal warning,

"Police have been alerted, police have been alerted!!"

A few minutes later we have 3 police cruisers pulling into the property. All with lights and sirens. We were sitting on the porch watching the action, when the police exited their vehicles and stated,

"Show us your hands."

Which we did. We then asked the officer to call Lieutenant Craig Webkie of the pistol licensing section. The first responding officer said that this was a test of the robotic dog program that is being funded by the Secret Service. We explained to the officer that we all will have official waivers when the new law goes into effect next month. Our first call was to Craig who got on the phone and told the officers that we are former Secret Service and show us all possible courtesy. The next call was to Angelo Paparelli of the Secret Service who sent pictures of the waivers he had for us to their phones and would email the chief of police all waivers for former Agents in Suffolk County. The cops were always nice and explained that this was a test run and did a pistol license check against the list of those that received the MARK and that is how we were discovered. So, the dogs were sent out to locate us and alert. Today's technology is amazing!!

Saturday, January 17th, 2032

Today was very cold, not a day that you want to be outside, so we made a fire and watched TV. Diana and I were on the couch and she was flipping through the stations, then she stopped. Reporters were reporting from outside our house last night. Unbeknownst to me, there was a film crew following the robot dogs when they came to our place. Now we were all over the News!!! I immediately called Frank and Dominic and told them to turn on channel 7, either watch it there or come to our house.

Did the newscaster bother to try and talk to us - Nope. They just ran with what they had and it didn't make us look good at all. The Reporter, Alice Donnolly, stated that the robodog program is a test program paid for by the Secret Service and implemented by local police departments. It is scheduled to go live next month when President Harris enforces the non-MARKED location program; in other words, anyone not having the MARK is to be located so that the government knows where they are. Alice went on to state that she followed the robodog's to our location and found out that 3 former Secret Service Agents lived here. Alice told the audience our names and gave out the property address. This isn't good. Dominic came over and said,

"We are going to have a problem."

I said,

"Let's watch the entire segment before we make our decision."

Not only did the reporter reveal our address, our names and the fact that we are all former Secret Service Agents. Alice went on to say that we had connections in the police department and that the Secret Service has granted us waivers for the law. Alice reported in such a way as to convey to the audience that we are receiving special treatment. Her presentation will sway some people to overreact and possibly protest at our property. I told Dominic and Frank that we need to monitor social media and see if anyone will want to try and make an example out of us.

It was a disturbing day but we ended it by cooking up some steaks and praying for wisdom.

Monday, January 19th, 2032

It didn't take long - Frank found a Facebook page dedicated to a protest at our property on Saturday January 31st at 4pm. People were pissed because the reporter made it sound like we were special, the exception to the rule. Why should we be allowed to get away with not taking the MARK just because we were Secret Service Agents?? In only 2 days they had 32 people ready to show up at our property to protest.

Frank was reading some of the posts and joined the chat under another name. Some of these people wanted to kill us. We all knew that we were in for a battle royale.

The three of us had a decision to make - how to defend and how much force to use. We all agreed that deadly force would be a last resort. We have to defend using buck shot, a .22 and tear gas, pretty much non-lethal. However, if the protesters show up with assault weapons, then we go to the next level with our own assault weapons.

Tuesday, January 20th, 2032

Now it's time to get to work. We have to plan this right. Based on the information we have so far, we are expecting about 100 people to show up and protest. Not to mention the harm they plan to us and the property. So, we made a list of what we needed to do:

1) We armed Farmer Ed with a semi-automatic shotgun and gave him plenty of buck shot. That should keep them away from his door.

2) We decided to dig trenches just past the automatic lights on certain parts of the property. So, we used the farm equipment to dig down about 4 feet and cover the trench with branches and leaves. We posted no Trespassing signs in front of each trench. So, if the protester violates the no trespass sign and then goes beyond the automatic lights as he continues, he will fall 4 feet into the trench. Listening to that person screaming to get out will deter others from entering the property.

3) We placed light explosives all around the property, these we can control through an app on Dominic's phone. This is a special app that we used on the job. We placed 24 of these around the property, more than anything they will be a deterrent. We used the minimum explosives possible to scare and not injure anyone.

4) Frank made sure the Ruger 22 and the Mini 14's was sighted in from 200 yards away. This gave us plenty of room for safety.

5) We called Craig at the Police department to let him know we may need some back up if things go sideways. However, there are a lot of police who hate us too because we didn't get the MARK.

6) We have our gas Masks ready, communications - walkie talkies and now it's time to practice.

Wednesday, January 21st, 2032

Today we brought out the Burna guns and tested where the tear gas would land firing from different locations. We figured that the biggest crowd would be on the street outside the gate so we practiced shooting from different angles so we knew where we had to be shooting from to hit our targets. At those points we set up barricades using cinderblock and sandbags. Once we set up barricades, we added storage for our gun safes so that each barricade would have a gun safe there in case it was necessary. We then practiced some drills to make sure that we are prepared when these protests begin. We got the communications down pat and practiced running out to the barricades and getting the Burna guns ready to shoot. We practiced using the explosives app and seeing how much of a blast it would cause. We reinforced the doors and put a protective covering over the windows. Over the next few days, we will perfect our response. When we were done, we took the time to pray and ask God for wisdom and strength.

Saturday, January 31st, 2032

Today is the day that the protesters come to our property. For the last few weeks all Frank, Dominic and I did was train and practice. We did everything from running to Jujitsu and kickboxing. We shot our weapons using low impact gun powder so the sounds would be muffled. We did whatever was necessary to be prepared for this day.

We were very fortunate the weather was warm for January, actually getting into the fifties. The day started at noon when Craig called from Suffolk County Police to inform us that a stand down order was in effect for tonight. The protesters wanted the police there to arrest us but Craig told them that we were undercover Secret Service and any police interference would lead to loss of funding from secret service and possible arrests to the officers. The Police Chief then called the Secret Service and ended up speaking to Angelo Paparelli and of course Angelo went with Craig's story and covered for us all. So, the Police Chief issued a stand down order telling the police not to interfere with us and if necessary, they will support us if we needed it. This is a huge win for us. The protesters were told that there were not enough police available to cover their protest. Some of the protesters who showed up at the police station were told that protesting at the home of former Secret Service Agents wasn't a smart idea. This seemed to dampen their enthusiasm, from what Craig told us.

At 3pm we geared up - bulletproof clothing. I put on a bulletproof sweatshirt and Frank and Dominic were wearing bulletproof jackets. We had guns and back up guns, plenty of ammo. We had the drones ready to take to the skies and shotguns and Burna guns ready to go. It was going to be a crazy night.

Frank came up with the idea of flooding the trenches. By doing so people will not want to hang around if they get wet. So, we took the hoses and turned them on, until we had about 4 inches of water in the trenches. This way if anyone breaches our property line and falls into the trench will get their feet wet, with the night air coming and the temperature dropping they will be forced to leave. After this we were ready for the protestors to show up.

At 4:35pm 2 buses pulled up outside the property. Each bus had about 30 people on it. We had binoculars so we could see them really well. They all got off the buses and they pulled out signs that were stored in the luggage compartment of the buses. The first sign read,

"Kill the haters,"

the second read,

"Everyone needs the MARK - No exemption to the Rule,"

and the third one read,

"Unity Religion or Die."

We knew immediately that it was going to be a crazy night. Frank took off for the sniper nest, he said that he will use the 22 Ruger unless it gets ugly then the .223 comes out. Dominic and I were in the main house and I put Diana in the hidden room out of harm's way; she had a walkie talkie so she could hear everything going on. I also trained her with my Sig 9MM and I gave her a backup 9MM plus 200 rounds of ammo, just in case.

The first hour was relatively calm after the 2 buses another 10 people showed up by car or truck so we had about 70 people total. They were just carrying the signs up and down the street in front of the property. Then it began to get dark. I mean in every way possible.

Dominic noticed one of the protesters go to his pick-up truck and pull open the gate to the truck bed and he had 6 five-gallon jugs of gasoline and 24 empty beer bottles. We radioed Frank and he put them in his sights. Dominic and I watched as they started filling the beer bottles with gasoline then cutting up rags and inserting them into the bottles to be used as a fuse.

I neglected to mention that we planted a camera with voice activation outside the property so we could see and hear everything. We could see there were 3 guys doing this. They were all dressed in black shirts and black jeans, not the nicest looking people. As they filled up the beer bottles and put fuses in them, they lined them up in the pick-up truck till all 24 were ready to go.

Then one of the 3 guys said to the other 2,

"Let's kill these Haters,"

with that he lit the fuse to a beer bottle filled with gasoline. I radioed Frank to shoot out the bottle and 1 second later that bottle broke in his hand and some of the gasoline splashed onto his pants and the still lit fuse fell to the ground. Then I told Dominic to get to the barricade and start using the Burna shotgun and put enough tear gas by that truck so no one can use those gas filled bottles. The guy with the gasoline on his pants shouted to the others,

"Grab a bottle and light a fuse."

Frank started shooting the bottles while they were still in the truck bed. Dominic started launching teargas near the truck to prevent anyone from using those bottles.

I radioed Farmer Ed and told him to get ready with the shotgun, I fully expected the protesters to rush to the house.

The crowd was stunned they didn't expect the tear gas or the sniper fire. Frank had shot up 10 of the beer bottles filled with gasoline and the gasoline was spilling unto the ground from the bed of the truck.

At this point a few protesters who felt the tear gas got onto the bus. But 6 others decided to come upon the property chanting,

"Unity religion or Die."

We warned them to stop but they didn't, they activated the automatic lights and just kept running. Without warning they dropped into the trench and started screaming,

"Help - get me out."

We warned others to keep off the property or their fate would be worse. All 6 of them fell into the trench and we could hear them drop into the water. Now they were all wet. Dominic placed a few tear gas rounds where they fell in. We could hear their screams get louder when they felt the effect of the tear gas.

The protest leader went onto the bus and came back with rope and got a few volunteers to help him get the 6 others out of the trench. They tried to call the police but were told that the police response time would be 2 hours and 30 minutes. In other words, the Police were not showing up to help them.

We patiently watched their every move. We let them help the 6 guys out of the trench. Then one idiot grabbed a beer bottle filled with gas, one of the few Frank didn't shoot out, and he lit the fuse screamed,

"Fuck you,"

and threw it. But as soon as it left his hand Frank shot the bottle and fire and gasoline ended up falling on the protestors and not us. This was the last straw for them. The leader of the protest told them to get on the buses and they did. The others who drove up in their own cars and trucks decided that it was time to go too.

By 9 pm no one was left. We sent up a drone to make sure and assess any damage to the property. We were very fortunate; it could have been much worse.

Sunday, February 1st, 2032

Today the new law went into effect - The MARK location law. We got waivers but it is almost impossible to live without the MARK. We can't buy or sell anything; we can't get services like medical care or lawn mowing. Soon they will announce rewards for turning people in and it will get worse but we know when the end will come so I will take a break from updating the diary for a while - till the war begins.

CHAPTER 31
ISRAEL INVADED

Friday, February 20th, 2032

After months of building up a 2,000,000-man army on the borders of Israel; the armies of Russia, Iran, Turkey, Libya and Turkmenistan, invaded the country of Israel today. They came in from 3 sides - Jordan, Syria and Egypt. Israel had to retreat. After the armies had gotten about 5 miles inside the country they stopped to regroup and set up camp. Then suddenly and without warning the greatest earthquake in the history of recorded earthquakes hit.

An earthquake that was so great that it could not be measured on the Richter scale. It killed hundreds of thousands of enemy combatants. This was God's last chance to show the nations that he alone is God and there is no other.

It seemed like it killed every soldier from the invading Armies but the Israelis lived. It reminded me of the miracles that God did in Egypt so, so long ago. All the equipment they invaded with was left intact and the Jews began to take their vehicles, supplies and weapons.

Saturday, March 6th, 2032

I turned on the TV to see the devastation the earthquake in Israel had caused. It was unbelievable - miles and miles of scattered equipment and dead bodies. Israel hired thousands of people to collect the dead and bury them in mass graves. They hired others to bring the military equipment to secure locations. People are saying,

"There truly is a God in Heaven."

Meanwhile, the Assyrian President said that this type of invasion can never happen again and said that he will begin peace talks with the Prime minister of Israel as soon as calm returns to the nation.

Friday, March 12th, 2032 7pm

The entire world watched as the Assyrian president met with the prime minister of Israel and presented him with a peace treaty. All the client states of the Assyrian President signed a peace treaty agreeing not to attack or invade Israel for 7 years with a renewal or extension of a year at a time after that. This was a great day for Israel and the world. Afterwards, the Assyrian president gave a press conference. He took credit for the earthquake, saying that since those countries were not under his control, they could be destroyed by this catastrophe, since he did not protect or defend those countries. He said that the invisible God of heaven could never do such a thing to the countries in his kingdom and spoke blasphemies against the god of heaven. The sad thing was to see the applause he received. Sad to see the world believe the lies of the Devil but he is such a good liar.

God will never be second to a created being so on this day Ezekiel 39:9 was fulfilled and the people of Israel began to use the weapons for fuel as a reminder of what God has done!!!

CHAPTER 32
CAUGHT UP

CAUGHT UP TO HEAVEN @11AM

Diana and I began our day in prayer then as we were praying at 11am we heard loud trumpet blasts and before we knew it, we were flying into the clouds, like a plane taking off. We flew through the clouds and into Heaven. Wow, what a glorious experience. Before we knew it, we were dressed in beautiful white clothes. We could feel the presence of the Lord as we entered heaven. Jesus welcomed us and said,

"Welcome to the marriage supper of the lamb."

Millions upon millions were there - praising God and giving him glory. We all knew from that moment on we would never be sad or cry again. We are the children of God, the chosen few that will be put in charge of his kingdom, when it arrives on earth 7 years from today. Diana and I will enjoy the feast but I may be tempted to write again and detail from heaven the events that will take place on earth during the last 7 years before Christ return, known as Daniel's 70th week (then the Kingdom comes!!!!).

This seven-year period of time begins with Daniel 9:27 when we see the Anti-Christ sign an agreement with Israel.

The Adventures of Bob and Diana may continue in my next book which will take place from heaven as the events of the last 7 years before the return of Christ unfold upon the earth.

In the second to last chapter of this book, I have provided a detailed listing of all the events that happen from the time the overcoming saints get caught up to heaven and the events of the tribulation period for the saints left behind. This will help you understand what the bible predicts.

Finally, the last chapter is about salvation. What the bible says about accepting Jesus Christ as your Lord and Savior.

CHAPTER 33
TIMELINE OF EVENTS

THE TRIBULATION PERIOD OF THE SAINTS - 1260 DAYS FROM THE RAPTURE TO DANIEL'S 70TH WEEK

I am going to list the main events from the Rapture, (or the time that the saints get caught up to heaven,) to the time the Anti-Christ signs the peace covenant in Daniel 9:27. From the time of the agreement begins a period of time known as Daniel's 70th week, it is the last 7 years before the Return of Christ.

Most prophecy teachers assume that this period of time occurs immediately following the Rapture but that is impossible since there is no war before the rapture so no need for a peace agreement. The war that leads to that peace agreement is seen in Ezekiel 38 and 39 and occurs more than 3 years after the rapture. The very moment that the Anti-Christ signs that agreement, Ezekiel 39:9 happens. God makes himself known to Israel through Ezekiel 39:9, he reminds them of what he did by letting the people of Israel use the weapons left over for fuel for 7 years, the exact same 7 years as Daniel's 70th week. This is why so much confusion hovers around bible prophecy. It's impossible to try and put ten and a half years of events into seven, it cannot be done. Once you understand this prophecy is easy.

1) The Rapture itself. This begins the 1260 day count down. Half of the believing Christians are taken up to heaven and half are left. The half that are taken are the Revelation 3:10 Christians - Because you have obeyed my command to persevere, I will protect you from the great time of testing that will come upon the whole world to test those who belong to this world. The ones that stay are seen in Matthew 25:

"All the bridesmaids got up and prepared their lamps. Then the five foolish ones asked the others, 'Please give us some of your oil because our lamps are going out.' But the others replied, 'We don't have enough for all of us. Go to a shop and buy some for yourselves.' But while they were gone to buy oil, the bridegroom came. Then those who were ready went in with him to the marriage feast, and the door was locked. Later, when the other five bridesmaids returned, they stood outside, calling, 'Lord! Lord! Open the door for us!' But he called back, 'Believe me, I don't know you!' So you, too, must keep watch! For you do not know the day or hour of my return."

2) This event causes massive confusion in the world and it begins the tribulation period for the saints that are left. This is the biggest biblical event since the Flood. It will totally change the world. It is this period of time that Jesus spoke about saying,

"And those who endure till the end will be saved";

he was talking about the end of the dispensation of grace. That is found in Matthew 24:13 (The other scriptures related to this are seen in Revelation 12:, Revelation 4:1, Matthew 25:1-13, Matthew 24:40-51; Revelation 3:10, 1 Thessalonians 4:16-17, 1 Corinthians 15:51-52, 1 Thessalonians 5:1-6, Acts 1:9-11).

3) A war in heaven takes place and Michael and the Angels fight against Satan and the demons and the demons and Satan are cast to the earth. It is at this time that Satan takes possession of the Anti-Christ and he seemingly comes back from the dead. (Revelation 12:7-13 and all of Revelation 13 tells the story.)

4) False prophet announces that the Anti-Christ is the true messiah and all should worship him. He calls fire down from heaven and orders a statue be built to honor him, this special statue could talk and appears to come to life. (Revelation 13:11-17)

5) The Anti-Christ speaks great blasphemies against God and demands to be worshiped forcing people to take a mark on their hand or head or they can't buy or sell!! For 1260 days he will persecute and kill the followers of Jesus Christ. He will take over Europe and many other countries, the entire world will fear him. The Muslims will hail him as their savior and chaos will rule the day. It is at this time when the love of many will grow cold and many false prophets will appear. (Matthew 24:10, Revelation 13 and Daniel 7:23-28)

6) Wars will break out like never before in human history. The Anti-Christ is constantly looking to enlarge his territory, first taking control of Europe then expanding to Africa and South America. Meanwhile, Russia, Turkey, Iran and several mid-eastern nations decide to Invade Israel. (Ezekiel 38-39,)

7) Anti-Christ and false prophet will ask for a one-world religion and one world government to bring everyone under the control of the Anti-Christ. This will cause great persecution for those that resist.

8) The Anti-Christ will mock God and exalt himself. However, the raptured saints will preach the gospel all over the world so everyone will hear it. (Revelation 12 and 13 details the story, Revelation 14:6 and Matthew 24:14)

9) Crime and lawlessness will be rampant. The Anti-Christ will encourage crimes against Christians and Jews. Christians will be arrested, persecuted and killed. Their homes will be burned; they will be beaten and raped.

There will be no justice for them because the world will consider their opposition to the new world order and one world religion evil. When these Christian saints die, they cry out to God in heaven for justice and are told to wait a little longer. Until the 1260 days are over. (Revelation 6:9-11, Matthew 24:9)

10) As a result of all these conflicts many people die in combat and inflation makes life unlivable causing famine and disease. It will take a day's wages just to eat. As a result of this 25% of the world's population will die during this 1260-day period of time. (Revelation 6:5-8)

11) There will be signs in the heavens - The Sun will become dark as Black Cloth and the Moon became Red as Blood. The stars will fall to the earth causing great distress. (Revelation 6:12-16)

12) Then the greatest earthquake of all time will hit Israel destroying the Armies of millions of men that came to invade the country. This is the last sign God gives man to repent before the end of the dispensation of Grace is over. At the time that this happens Israel has been invaded by Russia, Iran, Turkey and several other countries - they came to pillage and destroy but God had other plans. This is the event that precedes the peace agreement of Daniel 9:27 being signed and as soon as it is - Ezekiel 39:9 happens, the people of Israel begin to use the fuel of the weapons left behind for a total of 7 years, the exact duration of Daniel's 70th week as a sign that God is in heaven and still in control. (Ezekiel 38-39)

After these events Daniel's 70th week begins, it is the last 7 years before Christ returns. The agreement will be signed, the temple built, the Anti-Christ will proclaim himself God half way through the 7 years and the 2 witnesses will be sent down from heaven to proclaim the gospel to the Jews. The rest of these events is for my next book. However, if you are not a Christian, I encourage you to read the next and last chapter on salvation. Thank-you for taking the time to read this book, I hope you enjoyed it!!

CHAPTER 34
NOW'S YOUR ONLY CHANCE

HOW TO BECOME PERFECTLY ACCEPTABLE IN GOD'S SIGHT

You might be wondering why I would end a book about Bible prophecy (and the timing of Christ's Second Coming) with the importance of salvation. The reason is simple - your salvation, or lack thereof, will determine where you spend eternity. I want to do everything I can to help bring people to know the mercy and grace of God. It is his will for all to be saved and none to perish. However, it is your choice. God has already done his part. Christ died on the cross and rose on the third day. The rest is up to you.

Psalm 53

2 God looked down from heaven upon the children of men, to see if there were any that did understand, that did seek God.

3 Every one of them is gone back: they are altogether become filthy; there is none that doeth good, no, not one. NKJV

If this is true, then how can one become right with God?? The Bible gives us the answer in John 3:1-21.

There was a man named Nicodemus, a Jewish religious leader who was a Pharisee. 2 After dark one evening, he came to speak with Jesus.

"Rabbi," he said,

"we all know that God has sent you to teach us. Your miraculous signs are evidence that God is with you."

3 Jesus replied,

"I tell you the truth, unless you are born again, you cannot see the Kingdom of God."

4 "What do you mean?"

exclaimed Nicodemus.

"How can an old man go back into his mother's womb and be born again?"

5 Jesus replied,

"I assure you, no one can enter the Kingdom of God without being born of water and the Spirit. 6 Humans can reproduce only human life, but the Holy Spirit gives birth to spiritual life. 7 So don't be surprised when I say, 'You must be born again.' 8 The wind blows wherever it wants. Just as you can hear the wind but can't tell where it comes from or where it is going, so you can't explain how people are born of the Spirit."

9 "How are these things possible?"

Nicodemus asked.

10 Jesus replied,

"You are a respected Jewish teacher, and yet you don't understand these things? 11 I assure you; we tell you what we know and have seen, and yet you won't believe our testimony. 12 But if you don't believe me when I tell you about earthly things, how can you possibly believe if I tell you about heavenly things? 13 No one has ever gone to heaven and returned. But the Son of Man has come down from heaven. 14 And as Moses lifted up the bronze snake on a pole in the wilderness, so the Son of Man must be lifted up, 15 so that everyone who believes in him will have eternal life."

16 For God so loved the world that He gave His only begotten Son, that whoever believes in Him should not perish but have everlasting life. 17 For God did not send His Son into the world to condemn the world, but that the world through Him might be saved.

18 "He who believes in Him is not condemned; but he who does not believe is condemned already, because he has not believed in the name of the only begotten Son of God. 19 And this is the condemnation, that the light has come into the world, and men loved darkness rather than light, because their deeds were evil. 20 For everyone practicing evil hates the light and does not come to the light, lest his deeds should be exposed. 21 But he who does the truth comes to the light, that his deeds may be clearly seen, that they have been done in God." NKJV

There are three things that Jesus tells us in this scripture:

1. A man must be born again.

2. Jesus was going to die so that you may have eternal life.

3. God so loved the world, that he gave his only begotten son, that whosoever, believeth in him should not perish but have everlasting life.

God loves you and I so much that he sent his only son Jesus to die on the cross and then raised him from the dead. Through Christ's death, God offers you forgiveness for your sins; and through his resurrection, the promise of everlasting life. Christ died for the entire world, but whether or not we accept what he did is up to us. God gave us free will to accept or reject the sacrifice of his son, Jesus. Paul the Apostle talks about salvation in the book of Romans. It is one of my favorite books in the entire Bible, and I encourage you to read it. I will sum up the five main points here:

1. Man is sinful. Romans 3:23 says this:

For all have sinned, and come short of the glory of God.

2. Sin has a penalty. Romans 6:23 says this:

For the wages of sin is death; but the gift of God is eternal life through Jesus Christ Our Lord.

To continue in sin will result in spiritual death, which is separation from God forever. The alternative is to personally receive God's free gift, which is pardon for sin and provision of life everlasting.

3. Christ paid the penalty, Romans 5:8 tells us,

But God showed his great love for us by sending Christ to die for us while we were still sinners.

4. Salvation is a free gift. Ephesians 2:8 says,

God saved you by his grace when you believed. And you can't take credit for this; it is a gift from God.

Grace means undeserved favor. God graciously offers you what you could never do for yourself. God's gift to you is FREE! You do not and cannot work for a gift. All you need to do is receive it. Believe with all your heart that Jesus Christ died for you to provide deliverance from your sins and to give you eternal life.

5. We must receive Christ. John 1:12 tells us,

But to all who believed him and accepted him, he gave the right to become children of God.

When you receive Christ - when you accept what he has done for you - you become a child of God. Picture this if you will: Jesus Christ standing at the door of your life. Invite him in. He is waiting to be received into your life. I urge you to receive Christ now by praying this prayer.

Dear Lord, I know that I am a sinner and that I need your forgiveness. I believe that Christ died in my place to pay the penalty for my sin and that he rose from the dead. I now invite Jesus Christ to come into my life as my savior. I am willing to turn from my sin and live my life for you. Thank you for making me your child. Help me learn to please you in every part of my life.

Remember God's promise, which is found in Romans 10:13,

"For whosoever shall call upon the name of the Lord shall be saved."

EPILOGUE

God wants a relationship with people, not religion. The only people that Jesus criticized during his time on earth were the religious Pharisees and Sadducees. The reason was simple - they were more concerned about their religion than they were about their God. To prove this, God has sent us his Holy Spirit, also known as the comforter. John 16:7-13 says this.

Nevertheless, I tell you the truth; It is expedient for you that I go away: for if I go not away, the Comforter will not come unto you; but if I depart, I will send him unto you. 8 And when he is come, he will reprove the world of sin, and of righteousness, and of judgment: 9 Of sin, because they believe not on me; 10 Of righteousness, because I go to my Father, and ye see me no more; 11 Of judgment, because the prince of this world is judged. 12 I have yet many things to say unto you, but ye cannot bear them now. 13 Howbeit when he, the Spirit of truth, is come, he will guide you into all truth: for he shall not speak of himself; but whatsoever he shall hear, that shall he speak: and he will shew you things to come.

When you enter into a relationship with God, he will give you his Holy Spirit. Then you will know the goodness and mercy of God.

ABOUT THE AUTHOR

Michael Vilardi is a retired Criminal Investigator for the U.S. Treasury Department. He has studied bible prophecy since 1979, written several other books on the subject and had his own television show. Mike has a BBA in Accounting and an MBA in Management both from UMASS Amherst. He is currently an IRS Enrolled Agent. For more information visit:

www.MikeVilardi.com

www.ingramcontent.com/pod-product-compliance
Lightning Source LLC
Chambersburg PA
CBHW080543180626
46818CB00008B/3106